MW01248219

THE ART OF MADNESS

THE ART OF MADNESS

a novella

ELLA SHERRY

ISBN: 979-8-9908065-0-4 (Paperback)
       979-8-9908065-1-1 (Ebook)

Library of Congress Control Number: 2024910419

Any references to historical events, real people, or real places are
used fictitiously. Names, characters, and places are products of the
author's imagination.

Cover design by Ella Sherry.
Cover image: "Grandmother's Love Letters" by James Carroll
Beckwith, c. 1895.

Printed by Ella Sherry in the United States of America.

First printing edition 2024.

For everyone struggling with mental health—
you are not alone and you never will be.

She is too fond of books, and it has turned her brain.

—LOUISA MAY ALCOTT,
WORK: A STORY OF EXPERIENCE

I

The first week of November is cold.

The leaves have already turned, blowing in a breeze that ripples across campus. Georgian brick buildings pop up from between small clumps of evergreen trees, early afternoon light springing from one diamond-paned window to the next. The writhing academia from inside almost punctures the ivy-covered walls; the passion is nearly tangible.

Eloise is walking next to me, babbling about some class she desperately wants me to keep in my schedule. Her blonde braid falls down to the middle of her back and the green scarf wrapped around her neck complements it perfectly. If I didn't know she hates her hair I would be jealous.

I wave her off with a hand, shifting the books in my arms. She laughs—that high, shrieking laugh I've grown used to over the past year—and continues on.

"My God, Eloise," I sigh, "how much can you talk about one class?"

She grins. "I could talk for hours. I swear, you *can't* drop it, Henri. It's awesome. Come on."

"I don't know. My schedule is already pretty full." It's true—a basic creative writing class, philosophy, English poetry during the Romantic movement. I don't need to add art history on top of it.

"Well, just think about it, okay? It's fun. I'm sure you'd like it."

She turns her head and notices a group of boys standing off the dirt pathway, shouting at them and waving a hand. I duck my head and feel my cheeks redden. I've never been like Eloise and I never will be.

Her words are inaudible but that might just be because I can't hear over my own thoughts. Maybe I should take art history, I think. At least it won't be the same English lessons as last year, which my current schedule has me set up for. Maybe I'll get some new ideas to pull me out of this bout of writer's block.

I abandon my head for a moment and listen to what Eloise is saying. She's yelling at the boys about some trigonometry class she's taking and they shout back. They're exactly the kind of people I expect Eloise would be friends with: all sharp angles and classically poised, eyebrows at just the right tilt and hair that doesn't need to be constantly fixed. I run a hand through my frizzy curls.

Eloise groans. "They want me to give them the notes from yesterday."

"Now?"

"Now."

"Why don't they have them?"

She shrugs. "You know. They probably slept in too late or something and skipped class."

"So why would you give them the notes? Isn't it their fault they don't have them?"

I watch as she sets her jaw and places her hands on her perfectly curved hips. This is a stance I know well enough. I'm about to be lectured.

"Do you not listen to me, Henri?" she scolds. "You see that black-haired one, to the right? The one with the baseball hat?" I nod. She's gone over this before. "Well, that's Jackson. And Jackson happens to be in my astronomy class, too, and he has all the answers to the midterm because his sister took it two years ago, and Dr. Clayton never changes it. So, I kind of need to get on his good side, right? If I'm going to pass this class?"

"Right."

"So, don't you think giving him the trig notes from yesterday is a good way of getting on his good side?"

"Right."

"Are you even listening to me right now, Henri?"

No. I'm thinking about Portia's Act 4 monologue from *The Merchant of Venice*. I really couldn't care less about Eloise's astronomy class or how she's so obviously attracted to Jackson and won't admit it.

"Yes," I insist. "And I get it. Astronomy's hard. But I'm just saying—"

"I don't care what you're saying. I'm giving them those notes and Jackson's giving me those answers." She spins on her heel and starts to walk towards them, calling over her shoulder. "And you'd better keep the art history class!"

The level two introductory creative writing class is almost identical to last year's. We meet in a small classroom, sand-colored wood tables arranged in a circle formation. Chalkboards are on the walls at either side of the room and one of the walls is covered in windows. I count sixteen other people in my class. I don't recognize most, except for a few I've seen around campus. That doesn't say much—I'm not a very social person.

When the professor finally walks in, class technically started five minutes ago. He is short and stout, with a ring of hair on the top of his balding head and a long white beard. Glasses are perched judgmentally at the tip of his nose. He ambles up to one of the chalkboards and writes his name in a careful scrawl: Dr. Thomas O'Kelly. When he speaks he has a British accent.

"Welcome, class. My name is Dr. O'Kelly." He pauses for acknowledgement and proceeds. "I'd like to start off with a question: what is literature? No, literature's too broad a word. What is a story?"

The class freezes. I look around but each of the faces seem to be blank. Nervously, I raise my hand. The professor notices.

"Yes, Green Sweater."

I shift in my seat. "An experience?"

"Of whom?"

I frown and pause. "A human."

"Ah." The tips of his mouth curl upwards. "What about

all you historical fiction writers? You science fiction writers? Have you experienced those events you write of?"

I shake my head and interrupt. "But isn't all fiction grounded in reality?"

"Is it?"

"Well, it has to be."

"Why?"

I frown again. "Because, if it wasn't, it wouldn't be believable. The reader wouldn't trust the writer. There would be no point."

"Yes—but what exactly is the *point* of a story?"

A shrimpy boy with wire-rimmed glasses perks up. "To teach a lesson?"

"Yes, that's true," Dr. O'Kelly nods, a flicker in his dusty grey eyes. "Let's take *Lord of the Flies*. What's the moral? People are terrible. They will inevitably tear each other apart in the face of savagery. What about *The Picture of Dorian Gray*? People are selfish, people are egocentric. So I ask you again: what is a story?"

The class is silent. Early morning sunlight ripples through the classroom, the willow tree outside making it dapple off the numerous bookshelves behind where I'm seated.

Dr. O'Kelly does not sigh at the silence. His forehead wrinkles and he looks at each of us in turn.

"Power. A well-written story has the power to corrupt, or to save."

And then he starts passing out syllabi as if he hasn't just left seventeen nineteen-year-olds utterly speechless.

When I wake up the next morning my head is throbbing. I

groan, rubbing my forehead, but stand and pull on a sweater over my pajamas.

I walk out of my room and shuffle through the living area, grabbing a chipped mug from a cupboard. I'm too tired to make tea, so I reach for the only open beverage I can see: a cold jar of coffee from yesterday morning.

"Jesus," I mumble, taking a sip and plopping onto an orange leather couch that faces the window. My head and heart are pounding but I don't take notice, instead taking a face-down paperback from the coffee table. It's a copy of *One Flew Over the Cuckoo's Nest*, which I fortunately haven't read before.

I curl my feet underneath myself, pull a blanket over my legs, and open the book to page one, taking sips from the mug as I read.

One hundred pages in, my roommate, Clary, stumbles in. It's obvious she's just woken up—her reddish hair is piled in a heap of tangled curls on top of her head, eyes in slits and squinting at the light that breaks through the window.

She grunts a greeting and lurches into the kitchen, pouring herself a glass of water and coming to sit beside me.

"How was the party?" I ask, raising my eyebrows.

She groans. "Obviously good."

"Meet anyone?"

"A girl. A musical theater major." Clary always gravitates towards the dramatic ones. "She's pretty. Blonde hair, blue eyes."

"Hm."

I look at her and she gives me a grin.

"You just start that?" she asks, nodding to my book.

"Yes. About an hour ago. It's...It's good so far. Interesting."

"I wouldn't know." She pauses to sip her water. "I've never read it. Laurence brought it over the other day and never asked for it back."

"Ah. That explains the coffee stains."

Clary doesn't drink coffee. She prefers to write plays entirely un-caffeinated but with enough alcohol in her blood to burn down a whole building.

I look out the window and am reminded of my walk back from class yesterday, with the view of the trees that looked like they were on fire and a cloudless sky. It's going to be a warm day; I can tell. But suddenly a wave of discontent washes over me. I close my book and slide the blanket off my legs, angry at myself now.

Isn't this all I want? Someone to just sit and talk with, hands curled around coffee mugs, eyes crusty with sleep and the morning sun breaking through the November sky. How can I possibly be wanting for more?

I stand abruptly, tell Clary that I'm going to visit my mother in town. It's not a lie this time.

Haling's Cove may be only a college town but it houses the best coffee shop/bakery in the entire state of New York. Cove's Bakery (so creatively named) is tucked between the local bank and a liquor shop where most of the people at my school buy alcohol from. It has red and white striped awning and French windows with rickety metal tables and chairs pushed close, flower pots giving the illusion of a small garden.

The interior is reminiscent of an old Parisian bakery: detailed china in cabinets and small vases of lavender dotting

the furniture. The walls are all wood paneled, except for one —the wall with a tall cabinet is decorated with yellow wallpaper. I sometimes go to the café to sit and stare at the wallpaper as it changes patterns and the faces inside have long conversations with each other.

A mirror hangs behind the register (it doesn't take credit cards in an effort to remain nostalgic) with the day's menu scrawled in blue. Today's is pretty standard: croissants, baguettes, éclairs, macarons, madeleines.

I step up to the register, where a girl with dark bags under her eyes is slumped.

"Morning," she says, straightening. "What can I get you?"

"Um—two small coffees, a baguette, croissant...and two madeleines."

" 'kay. That's 18 dollars and 80 cents."

I grab a twenty from my pocket and hand it to her. "Keep the change."

She slides over a bag, filled with the pastries, and gives me two coffees. That's another thing I love about this bakery; there's never a wait for your order. I sling my arm through the handles of the bag and take the coffees with each hand.

My mom's house isn't far from the bakery. It takes maybe five minutes to walk, but I amble and finish my coffee before I even get there, so it takes a little longer.

I set down the bag when I reach the front door and knock. I wait a few moments before knocking again.

"Hello?" I call, tapping on the door for the third time. Normally she comes on the second knock. My mother's timid but she's not antisocial. "Mom? Hello? Are you home?"

After the fourth knock I take out my house key and open the door, lugging the bag and coffee alongside.

The house is exactly the same as when I left for college a year ago at the start of my freshman year. Tattered Persian rugs (probably fake); mismatched lights on the walls (probably from a garage sale); a wall full of books my mother has never read (probably stolen from the library she constantly visits); unwashed wine glasses in the sink (probably from last night, when, like every other night, she sat on the couch, watched cable TV, and drank two full bottles of wine—alone); a pile of records on the floor (probably junk my uncle keeps bringing over here and my mother doesn't have the heart to throw away); and cases upon cases of wine. I don't know where she gets those from, but I don't want my little sister to see them when she gets home from her sleepover so I shove them into the hall closet.

"Mom?" I shout again.

The house doesn't feel empty but I don't know where she could be. I check the bedrooms again and then the garage, but she's nowhere to be found. I go back to the kitchen, staring at the breakfast I've just bought for my mother, and sigh.

She doesn't have anywhere to go. Where could she possibly be?

"Mom?" I yell again.

It's then that I hear it—a small squeak, sneaker on tile, coming from the back of the house.

And there she is, sitting on the floor of her bathroom (the only room I didn't think to check, of course), head against the drawers, cradling an entire bottle of wine in her hands like a baby.

I pause to admire the drunken beauty of the scene: chin tilted upward, eyes in slits, clear sunlight making patterns across her forehead like some stained glass from a cathedral in Europe. If I were an artist I would sit down and paint her. But I'm not, and I can only stare for so long.

"God, Mom," I say when I see the stain on the rug. "What have you been doing?"

"Henri, dear," she slurs. "You're back?"

"Just for a few hours. I have a class soon."

"Aw, that's good of you, honey."

"How much have you had to drink? You know you shouldn't day drink, Mom, it's not good for you." I try to keep my voice calm and measured as I tear off strips of toilet paper, but the truth is she's starting to scare me. "Mom? How much?"

"Oh…" Her head lolls onto her shoulder. "I don't know…not much. Just this." She raises the wine with a hand and I can tell that it's empty.

"Really, Mom? You're telling me the truth?"

"Of course I am, honey. I never lie to you."

"Okay," I sigh, scrubbing the rug with the wet towels. "Mom, this is stained. I don't think it can come out."

"That's all right, honey. This rug needs to go anyway." She pauses, takes a breath. I stop and look up at her. "Did I ever tell you why we named you Henri?"

I start at the rug again. "Yes, Mom."

"Well, I'll tell you again. We thought you were going to be a boy, you know. Someone tall and strong like your father. Not that you aren't tall and strong. You are, we just thought it would be in boy form." She giggles. "Anyway, we decided on Henry for your name. Something timeless and unique"—

unique? In what world?—"and that we both agreed on, which is rare, you know. You remember our fights." I don't. I'm pretty sure I somehow blocked them from my memory. "So, we both liked Henry for your name. Thing was, we were so sure you were going to be a boy we never decided on a girl's name! So when you popped out, we didn't know what to do. Do we call you Henry? Do we change it completely? A nurse suggested keeping it Henry, just changing the spelling. And so that's what we did."

"I'm glad," I say.

"I'm sure you are. Henri is a perfect name. You know, when I was pregnant with you, I think I knew in the back of my head that something wasn't right. You were different, and it wasn't just that you were a girl and not a boy. No, you're different, Henri."

"Yeah, Mom. I'm going to get a shower started for you, okay? But I need you to go and pick an outfit, okay? From your dresser?"

"Oh, yes," she says. "I can do that."

"Can you get up on your own?"

"Yes, yes, dear," she insists, "don't worry about me."

She stands shakily, using the counter for support, but totters out of the bathroom without help. I stare off into space and get back to scrubbing the rug when I hear the front door slam closed and my little sister shout, "I'm home!"

"Dahlia!" my mom calls. "I'm in my room!"

"Hey, who brought this food? Mom, did you go to the bakery?"

"Yes, just for you!"

I roll my eyes and get another towel, listening carefully

for Dahlia's footsteps. She enters the bedroom and stops, presumably eating some of the food I just bought.

"Mom, what on earth are you doing?"

"Getting dressed, dear."

"What's on your robe? Is that wine, Mom?"

"I just had a little, Lia. Just while you were gone."

"That's not true, Mom. You're a liar. I saw the crates in the closet."

Crap. I perk up and lean against the door.

"Well, honey, there's no such thing—"

"If you say there's no such thing as too much wine I swear I will go kill myself." My mother quiets and lets her younger daughter talk. "I thought I told you to pick me up this morning. Where were you? I called but you didn't answer and Mrs. Jefferson had to drive me home. She has work, Mom, you know? Where she makes money? Jesus, I swear she's more of a mother to me than you are."

"Well, honey, I thought you said you wanted her to drive you home. You said I didn't have to."

"No, I *didn't*, Mom. I said *you* needed to give me a ride home. Are you stupid? I was so embarrassed because of you. You made Mrs. Jefferson late to work."

"I'm sorry, honey, I must have forgotten. I'll drive you next time."

"That doesn't fix it."

"Honey, I—"

"Whatever. I don't want to talk about it. Just leave me alone. And, God, Mom, don't leave the bathroom door closed."

I jump up and instinctively start trying to clean the rug. My sister opens the door and freezes when she sees me. She's wearing baggy jeans and a tight tank-top and holds one of the madeleines in her hand, half-eaten, eyes a dark forest green that shift around the room. She sees the wine bottle and connects the dots.

"That was for Mom," I say, nodding to the madeleine.

"What are you doing here? Shouldn't you be at school?" Red is creeping up her neck and I know she knows I heard their entire exchange.

"Shouldn't *you* be at school?"

"I'm skipping."

"Dahlia—" I want to tell her that she can't talk to our mother that way. But she juts out a hip and her lips fix into a pout and the words stick in my throat. "I have to go finish...a paper. Make sure Mom showers and gets into clean clothes. Please. And this rug can't be saved. You can just throw it out or donate it."

"Fine."

We don't say goodbye to each other. I leave in a hurry, forgetting all the pastries on the counter. By the time I remember I'm nearly at my dorm and can't handle going back.

I will my mind blank for a moment but it betrays me quickly, bringing back memories from last year and last summer: the sticky lemonade on the patio in the backyard, the bruises on my mother's face, Dahlia's purple knuckles, my lungs failing from underneath my heart every time she walked into the room.

My God I just want to leave.

Piles of leaves are on the ground next to the path I'm walking on, making little trenches that remind me of some fantastical war in a faraway land. The sun is high overhead and I check the clock on the tower of the on-campus church; it's 10:23. I'm late to my poetry class and I don't care.

I pull the sleeves of my sweater around my hands and grimace. I need to get out of here, away from Dahlia and my mother who I am terrified I will become and the wine stain on the floor of the bathroom and my goddamn head that won't let up from this morning.

My God I just want to leave.

So I escape the only way I know how. A cup of day-old coffee, a cigarette, a bleeding pen (and heart), and an open journal.

Adelaide Montgomery's father is dead. He's dead and she knows it. She lives next door to the library and hides underneath a pile of squash in the front yard. She's wearing a red rain jacket and crying. Her dirty blonde hair drips in rags beside her face, cheeks red from the cold. Next to her is a muddy teddy bear with buttons for eyes and a matted brown coat. The first memory she has of her father is picking mulberries by the creek. He gave her the muddy teddy bear. Rain reminds her of him, so she stays outside while the thunder booms and cries because she loves him.

Adelaide's mother staggers out the door, stopping at the steps of the front porch. Her white robe is getting wet because of the leaks in the wood awning but she doesn't care, because her husband is dead and now nothing is right and there's nothing she can do. She sees the bottle of champagne out in the road, slowly filling up with rain water, and makes no effort to get it out of the street before a car hits it. And a car does hit it: an old pickup truck with rusty mirrors and tires that desperately need changing. The bottle splits open into a million little pieces and sprays across the street. A few shards engrave themselves into the tower of squash but the woman isn't thinking about the possible harm that has just come her daughter's way. Instead she's watching the man in the car climb out and apologize profusely to her, explaining that he didn't see the bottle and will clean it up right away.

"It doesn't matter," she tells him. The harm has been done and there's nothing either of them can do.

He apologizes again and drives away. Then they're alone again, just a girl with honey for hair and a woman with needles for a heart. She could go inside and lock her daughter out, because her daughter looks so much like him and makes her want to scream at the same time. She could wrap her hands around the little girl's neck and squeeze until the breath fades away, but she's not a monster, she's just a woman with one broken lung and a heart like a champagne bottle. So she instead stays where she is, her hands gripping the splintery post of the porch as bits of wood dig deep into her palms. She tells herself she can't feel the pain—why should she (how could she?) when her husband is underneath thousands of rocks and pounds of dirt and there's nothing she can do except wait for them to bring the body out so she can cry over him once again and never stop. She could remember him, she could go to his favorite restaurant every night for dinner and buy her daughter her favorite meal, she could never give away his clothes to keep the smell of him in her house, she could never wash the car because that was the last thing she has that he touched, she could build a shrine with photos of him on her dining table, but she won't do any of those things because she's feeling selfish and the world hates her.

And Adelaide—Adelaide could throw herself into the street. But she knows the cars would see her bright red rain coat and slow before they reached her, swerving around her helpless body while staring and thinking 'god who is this girl, why is she crying and why does she have a teddy bear, she's so crazy she's so stupid what is she thinking?' Because the truth is she isn't thinking. She's feeling and she feels that she wants to be with her father. She feels that if she has to go back to another day of college without her father's weekly letters she might just throw herself into the road without thinking. And isn't that such a beautiful thing? A girl, driven insane with grief, throws herself into the street in a desperate effort to meet him again. She sees stories like that every day. Would it really be so wrong? 'Yes,' her father would say if he were here, 'yes it is so wrong, because you don't have to do something just because everyone else is doing it. You can—have you read that Jack Frost poem?' 'Yes, Dad,' she would say, 'everyone has.' 'You shouldn't follow other people for the sake of following them, Adelaide. You have power over yourself' but she doesn't really, because her mind and her heart are telling her to throw herself into the road.

So she sits underneath the squash like her father underneath the rubble, and she cries and cries and will never stop crying because her father is dead and she isn't.

"Now—now look at this," the professor says. He's scatter-brained and probably should be admitted to a mental hospital but he's one of the most engaging teachers I've ever had. "The Hagia Sophia. I know I'm skipping over thousands of years of history, but my God it's gorgeous. You see? Look—look inside, those columns, look at that. You can see it all, all the—This class isn't going to be about the cold hard facts. I want to talk about art and history as something you can appreciate and something you grow to love because it is absolutely necessary for the human experience. We build to express just as we write and paint and draw and sing and make music to express. We kneel under beings we believe to be greater than our feeble minds and we build monumental structures in honor of them because we are so caught up in the wonderment of it all, the wonderment that we are alive and shouldn't we leave some kind of mark upon this barren planet? And my God aren't we just spectacular. The pyramids of Giza, Versailles, van Gogh and Picasso and Kahlo, the Hagia Sophia, Stonehenge: we are so absolutely extraordinary and we must *produce*, we must *create* in order to demonstrate the beauty of us. Now, now look again—the Hagia Sophia was built originally as a Greek Orthodox church under the rule of Justinian the Great, but then converted into an Otto-man mosque. And look at how they changed it: covering up mosaics, adding Arabic calligraphy that still can be seen and admired today, an off-center mihrab that points to Mecca, four minarets. Look at all of this." He gestures to a photo he's projected onto the chalkboard. "Look at these stunning columns, look at the capitals on top, classical ionic, as you'll learn later, a classic Greek order, deeply drilled stone and a structure that visually contradicts the burden that is brought upon it. I say that again: the columns visually contradict the burden they are forced to uphold. We see that all over art, all over the world, a recent example being la Sagrada Familia in Barcelona, I'm sure you all know it, look at those columns inside and tell me they're not denying the weight of that church. Because this is art, this emotional connection to materials from the earth being made into something grander and something better. And it's something artists have been using since the beginning of time, since the first cave wall paintings before writing was even invented, and it's something that makes up the fundamental pillars of art. Emotional expression is art, I think I said that before, but that is what makes art deeply human. Now I know most of you are taking this class either for fun or to fulfill some requirement, but I want you to start seeing the *wonderment* of our species and the things we create. I'm going in circles now and I apologize for talking about seemingly random pieces of art in the first class but I wanted you all to get a taste of what it's going to be like so you can drop it before it's too late. Time is almost over, you're tired, I understand, now go and sleep or do whatever you do."

It's 11:30. Class is over, and the rest of the students, already packed, leap up from their seats and file out of the lecture hall with a chorus of groans. I stand and slide my notebook into my bag, mind still reeling from the professor's lecture.

I race out of the hall and run to Eloise's class. She's outside with a group of girls I've never seen before. I shout her name and she looks over, waving at me.

"I just wanted to say," I call, "thank you for convincing me to take art history!"

Her face breaks out into a wide smile, as if she could get any prettier. "You're welcome!"

She turns back to her friends and I leave again, ambling across campus with no real idea of where I'm going. When I round the corner of some colonial-style building I know I'm on the side of campus where most of the math and science classes are taught. I recognize my old calculus building and immediately grimace. Next to it is one of the few parking lots on campus. There are only three cars parked there: an old Mercedes, a BMW, and a Ford.

I see a group of students standing nearby—clearly science majors, because they're obsessing over trivial facts about the periodic table—and they're spotless: sharp jawlines, neat hair, elegant clothes, perfect grammar despite their disdain for English, organized notes. They aren't hunching over books like most of my friends; they have lightning-rod postures and have now moved on to talking about some math equation no one else understands.

I'm too busy staring at them until I stop walking—a door has appeared right in front of me. I step back and look up, the sign on the building alluding to a coffee place. I make a face but open the door.

It's cold inside, the air conditioner purring loudly even though it's a week into November. The floor is uniform with black and white tiles. The boy behind the register motions me forward with a skeptical look and asks for my order.

"Just a small coffee, please," I say. "Black."

"Is that all?"

"Uh—yeah. Thanks."

"You can charge it to your dorm card."

I pull out the plastic card used to enter dorm buildings and lecture halls, handing it over. He stares me down and hands it back, motioning to a little touchpad in front of me, next to the tip jar. I blush and enter the four-digit pin. He gestures over to the farther side of the counter and I walk over, thanking a girl who hands me a mug of steaming coffee.

When I turn around I scan the shop and spot an empty table by the window. I slide into a seat and pull out the book

I began yesterday. I pause to sip the coffee and look around the shop again. There aren't a lot of people here. Just two boys at the table near the door, discussing something over pastries and a notebook filled with writing, a girl sitting alone and reading a magazine, and a boy at the table beside me, also reading a book. I look at the cover: *Lady Susan*.

I look back down to my book and open it but don't read. Instead I'm still thinking about the lecture I just came from. My stare wanders over the café and eventually stops on the boy next to me.

He notices my gaze and meets my eyes, giving a small smile. My cheeks redden and I stare down at my book. He looks around the café as if to make sure no one's watching, and slides into the chair across from me.

"Hello," he says simply.

"Um—hi."

"I'm Theo."

"Henri."

He doesn't comment on my name like most people do. "What are you drinking?"

"It's just coffee."

"Black?"

"Yeah."

"Hm."

"Why are you reading Jane Austen?"

"Is there a rule against it?" he smiles.

"No, I just—I've never really seen someone else reading that book. Most people only read *Pride and Prejudice*, or *Emma* or something."

"I find it interesting." He pauses. "Aren't you in my art history class?"

"You're taking art history?"

"Is there a rule against that too?"

"Well, no. I just..."

"I get it. I thought it sounded interesting and I needed to satisfy the art requirement, so I decided to take it. The professor's a character, isn't he?"

"Yeah." I'm not surprised he's just doing it for credit. "You think a lot of things are interesting. Jane Austen, art history. What's your major?"

"Computer science."

"Oh."

He laughs, pushing back his hair at the same time. It's strawberry blonde, curly and falls almost like a mop on his head. His wire-rim glasses frame his eyes perfectly. I avert my eyes and close my book.

"What did you think about the lecture today?" he asks.

"Oh. I...I really enjoyed it. The professor's crazy, of course, but...to use your words, I found it interesting. My friend convinced me to take it—she's an art history major—and I was pretty resistant, but now I'm glad I decided to."

"I feel the same way."

There's a moment of awkward silence and I look up at the clock on the wall. It's almost one.

"Shoot. I have to go," I say.

"Oh, sure." He stands with me and I shove my book into my bag. "Henri, would you want to hang out sometime later this week?"

I raise my eyebrows, pushing a strand of hair behind my ear. "Like a date?"

He shrugs. "Maybe. Yes."

"Um...sure. There's a bakery in town. Cove's Bakery. I guess I can meet you there tomorrow, at 12, after art history? If you can."

"Sure, that works for me," he says.

Before he can say anything else I turn on my heel and leave the café, walking out into the considerably warmer air.

Adelaide gets a phone call from her next door neighbor one morning. She's in the middle of eating breakfast—soggy cereal she's just forcing into her mouth—and because she doesn't move from her seat in the living room, her mother huffs an annoyed sigh and picks up the phone for her. It takes only a moment for her to realize who it is and hold it out to her daughter.

"It's Archie," she says bluntly.

Adelaide, despite the weight in her chest, gets up and takes the phone from her mother.

"Hi, Archie," she says. "How are you?"

Over the phone, her neighbor gives a breathy laugh. "That's not a question for me, that's a question for you, Addie."

"Yeah. I'm okay. Well, sort of."

"As okay as you can be."

"Yeah."

"Listen, you know those turban squash I planted in my back-yard, around four months ago? They're ready to be harvested, and so I was wondering if you'd like to come over and help me."

"Oh. Right now?"

"If you're up for it."

"Um..." Adelaide looks back to her mother in the living room, picking at the string on a nearby pillow. "Yeah, sure. I'll be over in a minute."

"Great, see you then."

"Yeah, bye."

She hangs up and immediately walks to her room, slipping on a coat and shoes. She leaves without saying a word to her mother.

Outside is cold and the layer of fog that has rolled in almost blinds her red, puffy eyes. She steps onto the grass in her front yard and immediately feels her socks getting wet, grimacing slightly. Still, she continues on and turns to the right when she reaches the sidewalk, hair fully soaked through from the large droplets falling overhead.

Her neighbor Archie's house is almost identical to her own, except the fence splitting their yards is covered in vines and flowers, and the bushes in front of his porch are remarkably better kept. They're neat and even, while Adelaide's are overgrown and misshapen because her mother refuses to trim the ones in their yard.

She starts up the steps and onto the porch, wringing her hair out onto the wood. Beside her is a rocking chair and a statue of a dog. In the past Adelaide would run a finger along its porcelain ears but today she knocks on the door, wrapping her arms around herself in an effort to keep the cold away. It doesn't really work.

Archie opens the door quickly, as if he'd been waiting there for her.

"Hello, Addie," he says, ushering her inside. "I didn't realize it'd started raining again."

"Yeah," she says.

She slides her shoes off and steps inside, Archie closing the door behind her. He takes her coat and hangs it up on the door.

"I'll still need that," she says, "if I'm going back out to the squash."

"Oh, no, no, no," he says. "It's raining too much now. You'll catch a cold if you go back out."

"But—"

"It's fine, Addie. Really. The squash can wait."

He gives her a half-smile and she tries to return the gesture.

"So. Would you like some tea?"

Adelaide wants to say no—she doesn't like tea—but she finds herself nodding her head and following him to the little kitchen.

The house used to be organized and methodical when Archie's wife was still alive, but in the ten years since he's let it fall into a state of collaged disorder. Newspapers are haphazardly strewn on the floor, some probably years old. Adelaide spots at least four full coffee mugs sitting on nearby tables. And of course his grandchildren's drawings are taped up everywhere because he can't seem to get enough of crayon-colored stick figures.

The kitchen is even more of a mess but Adelaide doesn't comment on the piles of dishes in the sink. She reminds herself to come back here to clean up a little, just after she gets past these first few days of grief.

Still, despite the chaos, Adelaide's heart rests for the first time since her mother told her about what had happened. An expected wave of calm washes over her.

"Sorry for the mess," Archie says, waving a hand in the air. "I try to clean it up, but then I'll find something else I need to do and on and on. I can never seem to get anything done." He chuckles and opens a cupboard, grabbing two mugs.

Adelaide somehow finds a tea kettle and fills it with the tap water, placing it on the stove when it's full. Together, they flinch when the kettle begins to hiss but Adelaide quickly pours the boiling water into their two mugs, and they wait as the water darkens into tea.

Once the tea is done, Archie gestures for her to sit down at the dining table in the next room and he brings the mugs out and places one down in front of her. She smiles in appreciation and ignores his groans as he lowers himself into a seat.

She takes a sip but doesn't spit it out. It takes everything in her to not grimace.

"You're quiet, Archie," she says.

He shrugs. "You don't look like you want to talk about anything right now."

"Oh."

"When does your school start up again?"

"Next week."

"Will you go back?"

"I don't know. I don't really want to."

"You should talk to your mother about it. She might understand."

They look up at each other from their teacups and stare. They both know Adelaide's mother most definitely won't understand.

Theo isn't in the lecture hall when I arrive for art history. The professor isn't either, but I assume he's the type of person who's always running late to his own classes.

I settle into my seat and take out a notebook from my bag, looking over my notes from the last lecture. It's scattered and barely coherent—phrases pop out at me; "kneel under beings we believe to be greater than our feeble minds," "visually contradicts burden," "so caught up in the wonderment of it all."

And then, at the very bottom, scribbled in red pen: *shouldn't we leave some kind of mark upon this barren planet?*

The door slams shut and I look up. It's the professor, dressed in a floor-length coat with cowboy boots. A few snickers emerge from around the room but no one's brave enough to actually say something.

"Well, good morning," he says. "I apologize for being so late. I assumed a large number of you wouldn't be in class today." He pauses and lets us murmur. "I'd assumed I scared most of you off." Uneasy laughter. "I suppose it's positive that you've chosen to stay. Well, let's get on with it, then. I know yesterday I went extremely out of order, with the Hagia Sophia and mentioning the Sagrada Familia. I'd like to start this class off in the order that the works have been created. We will start with prehistory, and continue on up until this very year. Now, can anyone tell me what our first work is, if you looked over our textbook?"

The class is quiet and he smiles.

"That's quite alright. We will begin with the Apollo 11 stones." He walks over to a table near the middle of the hall and switches on the projector, pulling up images of flat, cracked rocks with a dark sketch of what appears to be a leopard on them. "Found in Namibia and dating from around 25,500 BCE, this stone is among one of the first known recorded works of human art. So, most works from this period were two dimensional. Humans at the time weren't as intellectually advanced and their art reflected that. Their art was typically associated with food, settlements, animals, status, or burial rituals. And the function of these stones, the Apollo 11 stones, is unknown. Many works from this period have unknown functions and patrons. It's suspected that they were used for shamanic rituals."

The class drones on for another two hours. We cover ten artworks in that period, going surprisingly fast. I would have thought that the professor would take at least an hour on one artwork, but he seems to be speeding through them. Towards the end of class he admits why.

"To be honest, class, I don't enjoy prehistoric art. It's fascinating, yes, but there's so much that is unknown it gets rather repetitive. Now, I'm going to let you all go. Remember to go over your notes from this lecture before next class, please."

The class shuffles out the doors, spilling into the hazy afternoon light. It's almost 12, I realize. The professor went over the class time a little, and Theo must already be at the bakery.

I pick up my pace and shove my papers into my backpack, dodging groups of people on the pathway. I know I'm kicking up fallen leaves but I don't care.

By the time I get to the bakery, it's five past 12. I rush in and see Theo, sitting at a small table near the window with two small cups of coffee and two croissants. He sees me and smiles, waving. I ignore the fluttering in my chest and walk over.

"Hey," I say. "Thanks for...this. Sorry I'm late. You weren't in art history?"

"Yeah, I slept in too late."

"Oh. Well, you didn't miss much." I take a sip of the coffee, still burning hot. I feel it go all the way down to the pit of my stomach and grimace.

"Really? I thought you said you liked it."

I shrug. "I thought I did. Maybe not anymore. It's not that cool, I guess."

He frowns. "Right. Maybe it's just the art so far."

"Maybe."

I cross my legs under the table and look around the bakery. It's mostly empty, only an old lady with a small dog sitting near the entrance. The workers are whispering behind the counter and cleaning the coffee machine.

"So...what about you?" Theo asks. I look at him.

"What about me?"

"What are you like? What are your interests? Your goals?"

I shift uncomfortably. "Um...I like reading. Obviously, I'm a literature major. I like writing too."

"Oh, that's cool. Are you writing anything now?"

"Yeah, a novel."

"What's it about?"

I eye him. "You're not going to plagiarize me, right?"

He laughs. "No."

"I actually started it recently. It's about...I'm not really sure yet. But a mother whose husband just died. And she kind of...hates her daughter. She's jealous of her, and the daughter looks a lot like the husband, so the mother kind of wants to kill her." When I see the look on Theo's face I pause. "It's dark, I know."

"No, that's...well, yes, it's dark, but it sounds interesting."

"Hm. What are your hobbies, then?"

"I mentioned yesterday, I think, that I'm majoring in computer science."

"Yeah."

"Well...I like coding, and stuff. Graphic design. Basically anything that has to do with computers, I'm in."

"So...video games?"

He raises his eyebrows and takes another sip of coffee. "You caught me."

"No, that's cool. I've never really played any before."

"Maybe I'll teach you."

I laugh. "Maybe. Do you have any pets back home?"

"Oh. Um...I have a cat. Here, though, not at home."

"What?"

"In my dorm room. I have a cat. His name is Gopher, and I got him when I was a junior in high school. He was just a kitten then, but he's around the same size."

"Wait, wait, hang on. You have a cat? In your dorm room? Is that even allowed?"

"Technically no." He smiles mischievously. "But I didn't want to leave him behind. My family lives in Wyoming. It's pretty far and..."

He trails off, face reddening.

"Theo? It's far and what?"

"Well, we don't have the money to fly me back. I got here on scholarship."

"Oh."

He smiles. "Yeah. What's your family like?"

I gulp down another burning sip of coffee and shift my legs again, pushing a strand of hair behind my ear. "I have a little sister. Um...she's okay. I guess all little sisters can get annoying. I just—well, it's nothing. Sorry."

"No, I get it."

There's another quiet moment. I stare off into space behind

Theo, at a large cabinet filled with blue and white china. The window panes are dusty, with fairy lights hanging from the tops of the shelves. My eyes drift to the side at the yellow wallpaper. It's sort of an ugly pattern and color, mustard-like and splotchy. I've been tempted to ask the cashier multiple times who their designer was for this place but I've always chickened out.

I used to come in here and write all the time when I was in high school, and that habit hasn't left me since I graduated. There was a time when I didn't come for a month or two, though. That was after I first saw the wallpaper begin to change.

It's not dangerous or threatening or anything, it just swirls. Kind of like water.

"So," Theo says. "Where are you from?"

"Oh. Here, actually. My mom lives nearby."

"Oh, really? That's pretty nice. You must get to visit a lot."

"Yeah. It is nice."

I look down at my watch and knit my eyebrows together. A part of me feels bad that I want to leave, but another part of me desperately wants to just get out of this awkward situation.

"Hey, Theo?" I say.

He looks up from his coffee.

"I kind of forgot that I offered to help my mom clean out her garage today."

"Oh. Do you have to go?"

"Yeah, I think so. I'm sorry. I just—"

"No, it's okay. I understand. I do the same thing all the

time." He sets his mug down and readjusts his glasses. "Do you want me to walk you there?"

"No," I say a bit too loud. I clear my throat. "I mean, her house is close. I can just walk there myself."

"Oh. Okay."

"Yeah, sorry. Sorry."

"No, I understand." He stands with me, grabbing his coat from the back of his chair.

"But I'll see you in class later this week," I say.

"Yeah," he says, pushing his hair back with a hand. It falls back onto his forehead and a strand settles over his wire-rimmed glasses.

"Thank you for this," I say, gesturing to the coffee and croissants. "I had a lot of fun."

"I did too. Would you want to do something similar again, maybe?"

"Definitely."

"Okay. I guess I'll call you. Do I have your number?"

"No," I laugh. He hands me his phone and I put in my number, giving it back once I'm finished.

"I'll call you."

"See you later. Bye."

"Bye, Henri," he says.

I leave the bakery and make my way down Main Street and turn right, down a neat road with picture-perfect houses. As I walk, shame starts to flood my head. What on earth was I thinking? My first date ever, and I bail halfway through it. It wasn't even that awkward, thinking back on it. And I genuinely liked Theo.

I struggle with this realization and instead focus on the

nearby houses. The freshly-mowed front lawns are surrounded by spotless white fences, with a line of flowers in front of each and a willow tree in every yard. The only house that doesn't match is my mother's. The fence hasn't been painted in years and the wood is showing underneath. The grass in the front lawn is yellowing and the tree has been cut down.

I sigh and prepare myself for what I might face inside, although Dahlia probably isn't home unless she's convinced my mom to stay home from school. And knowing her, she most likely has.

I open the gate and walk up the little stone pathway leading to the entrance, knocking on the door.

"Mom? Are you home?"

It only takes a second knock for the door to open. My mother is behind it and her face breaks into a smile.

"Henri! Hello! What a wonderful surprise."

Her hair is tied up in a bun at the nape of her neck and she's wearing a green velvet dress with a large, gold statement necklace my dad got her for Christmas one year. I notice that she's not wearing socks with her shoes, but her face is unharmed and clear so I ignore any judgment related to what she's wearing.

"Mom? Are you going somewhere?"

"Oh, no, dear," she says. "I just felt like dressing up today. Come in, come in. My, it's chilly outside, isn't it?"

"Yeah," I say, stepping into the threshold and untying my scarf. "What are you doing?"

"Oh, you know. Just looking at old photo albums. Would you like to see?"

She doesn't really expect an answer, because she grabs my

hand and pulls me into the living room. On the coffee table are stacks upon stacks of photo albums from before Dahlia started high school—when my father was still living with us. My mother throws herself to the ground, back against the couch, and pats the floor beside her. I sit too.

"Look at this one, Henri," she says. "That was Easter Sunday, six years ago." It's like she's memorized the entire album. "We were all so happy then. Look at you! Just a little baby."

"I was a freshman in high school, Mom. That was a long time ago."

"Yes, yes. But look at Roger." She points to my father. "Look at that beard! I remember, I asked him to shave it off, because it was so scratchy. I hated kissing him because of it. Oh, that's not true. I loved kissing him."

"Mom," I say.

"I know, I know. Anyway, how's school?" She flips the page as she waits for me to answer.

"Oh, it's...it's good. I went on a date, actually, before this, and—"

"Oh, look at this one!" she exclaims. "We were all at Dahlia's piano recital, do you remember that, honey? She played something from the Nutcracker, I remember. Everyone was so impressed."

I let out a breath and my chest deflates. "Yeah, Mom. I remember."

"She was wearing that little green dress—green was her favorite color. But not dark green, she said, only minty green because it was a softer color. I thought it represented her really well."

I repress a snort. My sister isn't soft.

My mom gives me a glance from the side of her eye and smiles again. "Well, honey, I wish you had worn dresses more often. And not so much brown, dear. It really takes away from your complexion."

"Right."

"I mean, you're even wearing brown right now. Why not another color?"

"Because I like brown, Mom. Nothing's going to change that."

"It's the color of dirt."

"And what's wrong with dirt?"

"Nothing, dear."

"Hm. Is Dahlia home?"

"Oh, no. She went to school a few hours ago."

"Did you drive her?"

"Yes."

"I know I've asked this before, but isn't she sixteen? Why doesn't she have her license?"

"Well, honey," she says, closing the photo album and stacking it nearby, "not everyone prioritizes driving over school."

"I'm not saying she should, I'm just saying that it's been a while and—"

"Your sister is a wonderful person, Henri. Does it matter if she has her license or not?"

"No, I just thought that she would want more freedom, because—"

"Because what, honey?"

"Never mind. It doesn't matter. I just think you might want to encourage her to, you know, get it. She'll be a lot happier if she doesn't have to depend on other people for rides."

"Of course, honey."

She stands and starts to carry the albums out of the room.

"Mom? What are you doing?" I call.

"Oh, I thought I would maybe move these over to my room for tonight. In case I want to look at them later."

"Do you want me to help?"

"No, no, that's alright, Henri. You stay there. Actually, could you make us some tea?" She's shouting now that she's at the back of the house. "We can sit in the kitchen and talk about your day."

"Sure, Mom." I stand and make my way over to the kitchen, slipping out of my coat and tossing it over a nearby chair. I open a few cupboards, looking for the tea; it seems that my mother has rearranged the entire kitchen since yesterday. Finally, I find it, in the cabinet under the sink. "Hey, Mom, what kind do you want? You have peppermint, green, English breakfast, and black."

"Peppermint, please!"

I get to work, methodically boiling water and pouring some into two mugs from a nearby cupboard. I slide two tea-bags into the mugs and carry one out to my mother, back in the living room, bent over photo albums.

"Mom? Tea."

I hand her a mug that I remember Dahlia painting in elementary school. It's a normal size, originally white, but Dahlia painted little flowers with all of the colors of the rainbow across the sides. There's a small dog in the corner, its tail standing upright and ears flopping over the sides of its face. I try to remember what she was like when she painted this. Surely it wasn't the same as how she is now.

I scold myself as I sit on the couch and curl my feet underneath me.

My mother sips her tea quietly, stopping only to point and give a little exclamation when she sees a photo she particularly likes. I notice that they're mostly of us as a family: Dahlia, Mom, Dad, and me. On a hike, in a darkly-lit restaurant, at the beach. If she wasn't my mother I would hate her for it. Clinging to the past is not something I find admirable.

Adelaide does go back to college despite her attempts at convincing her mother not to. The fights were extreme, both women screaming and exhausted. Adelaide pitted her poor dead father against her mother ("He would have let me stay home if something like this happened," she had said. "You don't understand me! He did! He would let me stay home!"). But in the end she got into a taxi and rode across town to the little college on the lake.

Her mother always wins, she thinks. No matter what. She picks at the carseat and avoids conversation with the driver, who just wants to talk about the terrible storm that's about to come and how she should really buy some sandbags for her room if she doesn't want it to flood.

She's thinking maybe she won't buy sandbags, because maybe the room will flood and maybe she'll be asleep when it happens, unable to do anything. Maybe she'll wake, gasping for air, but choke on a breath of water, eyes closing with relief as she floats up to the ceiling like in a character in a tragic film.

She's always always wanted to be in a movie.

While Adelaide is thinking about rainwater and bubbles, her mother is at home, staring at the mirror on her vanity, deciding which lipstick is appropriate to wear now that she's a widow. The dark red? Mourning, but still alive. Pink? A retaliation against grief, convincing the world that she is still here and well. She chooses chapstick instead.

Now for the clothes. She could wear all black, but all of the women with dead husbands in town are unoriginal and their wardrobes consist entirely of black dresses. She wants no pity, so she opts for a bright yellow summer dress, even though it's 50 degrees outside and the front lawn is flooding.

She needs to take the squash away from the side of the road. They're probably dirty and inedible after being there for days, but she has nothing else to do. She slips on rain boots and leaves her shoulders bare.

When she steps outside she's met with a blast of freezing cold air. The air is damp and heavy. She trudges forward, down the stairs of the porch and wades through the 2-inch deep layer of water over the grassy yard. The stack of squash has toppled over from the wind and she heaves them one by one into a little red wheelbarrow her husband bought one day for the Fourth of July. Her tears mix with the rain.

She wipes her forehead and knows the people in the passing cars are staring; why wouldn't they be? A woman wearing a bright yellow dress soaked in rain, carrying squash to a bright red wheelbarrow. She almost laughs but then remembers she's supposed to be grieving.

By noon she's brought all of the squash to the porch, and walks inside without taking her boots off. The wet footprints will keep her company, she decides.

A knock sounds on the door. She pauses, unsure if she should answer or pretend she isn't here. The person raps the door again, this time calling her name.

"Henri? You there?"

I snap my head up and shut the computer screen, cocking an ear towards my door.

"Henri? Are you in there?"

Smiling, I leap up and rush to the door of my room.

"Hey," I say when I see Theo. "Sorry. I was writing, and I kind of get into the zone. It's hard for me to snap out of it. Did Clary let you in?"

"Yeah, she seemed kind of tipsy, though."

I laugh. "Oh, yeah. Probably. I think she was trying to write." I look at him, unable to express what I'm feeling. "How did you find our room?"

"I asked Eloise," he says with a lopsided grin. "Listen, it's raining out now, but I was wondering if you wanted to hang out or something." He peers into my dark room. "That is, if you're not busy writing."

"No, I was just finishing. Let me get a sweater and shoes, though."

He nods and wanders back out into the main space, making his way over to the messy piles of books near the window. I scramble to my closet, tossing on a brown sweater and a pair of shoes. I look back out—he's engrossed in the books—so I pull a brush through my tangled hair before closing the door behind me.

"Ready," I say. "Where are we going?"

He shrugs. "No idea."

We leave the dorm building and step outside. It's windy, cold, and frightfully rainy. The quad is scattered with brown and orange leaves, the trees stripped bare. Winter is coming.

"So...what exactly is your plan?" I ask.

He looks at me, grin on his face. "You seem like the kind of person who likes rain."

"To a certain extent. I like rain because it means I get to stay inside and read all day with coffee and a warm blanket. I don't like rain when I have to go to class or buy food."

"And what's your opinion on dancing?"

"Dancing? Why—"

"Just answer the question."

I pause. "I'm not a huge fan."

"No?"

"No. Why?"

"Because," he says, grabbing my hand and sending a rush of blood up my arm. "I want to dance."

"You want to—"

He pulls me out into the open, laughing when I squeal and try to cover my hair. As his blond hair gets drenched, it turns almost light brown, plastered to the sides of his face. I watch as he tilts his face upward, letting the droplets roll down his face while he opens his mouth, sticks his tongue out, and tastes the rainwater in a carefree manner I could never emulate. It reminds me of my mother in her bathroom—a strange kind of drunken, primal beauty but this time it's completely sober and happy.

His hands grip mine, butterflies rattling my stomach, and he spins me in a circle, still looking upwards. I laugh nervously and slow us down, fully aware there are a few people still walking around outside and giving us funny looks.

Theo notices my concern.

"Hey, what's wrong?" he asks.

"Oh—nothing. Just...people are staring, kind of."

I glance up at his face. He frowns and small droplets of water fall from his eyelashes. His glasses are all fogged up, sliding down the edge of his nose as he pushes it back up with the back of his hand.

"Does it matter that they're staring?"

I hesitate. "No, I guess. I just don't like it when people..."

"When people notice you?"

I force a laugh out, pushing a wet strand of hair behind my ear. "I guess so."

"Can't you just ignore it? Them, I mean?"

"It's not that easy," I say, raising my voice above a thunderclap. "I can't just let go of everything."

"Why not?"

"Because—" A bolt of lightning rattles my core. "Because I care too much."

He shrugs, letting go of my hands to wander farther away by himself. I follow desperately and hate myself for it.

"So what?" he says. "So you're just going to be miserable for the rest of your life, always wondering what other people think of you? What kind of a life is that?"

I stop walking. "Mine."

He pauses, turns around. "And do you like it?"

A warm breath escapes from my mouth. "Of course not. Look, it's not important. It doesn't matter. I don't really care. Can we just go back inside, because I'm freezing and completely drenched?"

He laughs and nods. We both cover our heads with our hands despite already being soaking wet, and race to the porch of my dorm building. Theo stops, shaking his head out like a dog, and a wave of sadness washes over me: this could be normal. *I* could be normal for once. Because there haven't been voices, not since the start of this school year, and maybe Theo is keeping them away.

But I know I'm wrong. This can never work. It never has and Theo isn't any different.

"What are you thinking about?" he asks, now squeezing water from his jacket. He pushes his glasses up on top of his head.

"Don't ask that," I say, "I hate that question."

He raises an eyebrow. "How come?"

"It's impossible to describe everything I'm thinking."

I watch as he stoops down and pulls off a shoe, flipping it upside down and staring at it while water pours out. He looks up at me and we laugh.

"Can I read what you're writing?"

"Oh. Yeah, no, sorry."

He laughs uncomfortably. "Why not?"

"I'm still on the first draft. It's pretty terrible."

"I don't care."

"You can read my finished stuff, okay? But if you read it now you'll be amazed at how mediocre of a writer I am, for someone studying literature."

"I don't believe that," he teases. "I bet it's incredible."

"You seriously do not understand my process of writing."

"I seriously do not."

He shakes his head out again and wipes off his glasses with wet sleeves, only smudging the water across the lenses. The yellowish light on the porch flickers on and off. Fog closes in on campus.

"I should go back up," I say, nodding to the building.

"Back up? Why?"

"Well, I have to write."

"Isn't it lonely, shutting yourself up all day? Don't you miss talking to people?"

"I talk to people. I talk to Clary. And you. And my characters."

"You're avoiding my first question, Henri."

"Fine, yeah, it's lonely. But that's the price I pay, I guess."

"The price you pay for what?"

"For being alone."

"What?"

"You can't be alone without being lonely. It just doesn't work that way."

"Henri, no. Who told you that?"

I shrug. "Myself?"

"No, Henri. You can be alone, but that doesn't mean you have to be lonely."

Shifting my weight to my other foot, I pause and look at him for a moment.

"Since when are you so wise?" I ask.

"Since always," he teases. He pushes his hair back again and looks off into the trees. "But I should probably go too. I have some work I need to finish."

"Okay. Bye, then."

"Bye," he says. He turns away, about to walk off, but then looks back. "Hey, there's a party someone I know is hosting. In the other dorm building. Would you want to come with me? It's this Wednesday."

"Wednesday? Someone's throwing a party in the middle of the week?"

"Well..." He grins. "Yeah."

"I guess so."

"Great. I'll come here at 8-ish and we can walk over together."

"Yeah. Okay."

"See you later."

He adjusts his glasses slightly and walks away, his steps light and playful. I stand outside on the porch until the fog swallows him up and I can't see him anymore. I squeeze water from my hair and open the door to let myself inside.

Theo arrives at exactly 8 PM on Wednesday night. I hear him come in, assuming Clary left the door unlocked when she left for work, and walk around the common area of the dorm room. I shut my book and open the door.

He's crouching by a nearby stack of books and looks over when I walk in.

"How on earth did you guys get this nice of a dorm room? It's huge."

"You were here a few days ago," I say. "You didn't notice how big it is?"

"Not really."

I smile. "It's because of Clary. Her family is really rich. I think her dad donated money to build this dorm building, and I guess the school was super thankful so they let Clary take her pick of the rooms, so of course she picked the best one. And she got to choose her roommate, too."

"And she chose you?"

"You say that like it's hard to believe."

He immediately backtracks. "No, I don't mean that, it just seems like you guys are so different and wouldn't really get along very well."

"We had a seminar class together last year." I shrug. "I guess I was one of the few friends she had before she switched majors. Now she's all popular with the performing arts people."

"Right," he says. "Are you ready?"

"Yeah."

The walk to the other dorm building is short—barely two minutes. Neither of us talk on the way there, but I can hear the music already rattling the ground. I sneak a glance at Theo, confused at how he knows people who would throw this kind of party. He doesn't seem like a social person, but his friends certainly do.

Inside of the building is even more chaotic than it sounds from outside. It's so crowded it's hard to stay with Theo, and we eventually lose track of each other. The room shakes with the sound of summer pop, although it's below 60 outside and the leaves are a fiery orange. The kitchen is lit with purple neon lights and a group of students are re-filling their red solo cups. Some colorless drink from a pitcher.

I spot Eloise in one corner, holding a cup to her cheek as she talks to a group of boys. I want to roll my eyes at her but instead push my way over and shout her name over the music.

"Eloise!"

"Henri, hi! I didn't know you were coming."

"I didn't either. It was kind of last minute."

"Oh. Cool! Well, it's fun, isn't it?"

I grit my teeth as someone runs into me, making me lose balance. "Yeah," I say. "It's great."

The boys around her slowly disperse and she notices, shooting them puppy-dog-eye looks. They laugh and shrug and continue walking away.

"Sorry," I say to Eloise. "I didn't mean to scare them off."

She laughs, that high, shrill laugh I hate. "It's fine. They were boring anyway. So, how's it going? I feel like I haven't seen you in forever! How's art history?"

"It's actually pretty interesting."

"I knew you'd like it! I told you, remember? I said you absolutely have to take that class, because it's so much fun. And the professor is insane, isn't he?"

"Yeah," I say. "I think it's funny that he didn't really tell us his name during the first class, like most of the other professors."

"Oh, he did that for us too," she says breathlessly. "I literally had to go back to the class description to find out what his name was."

I don't comment on why she didn't take notice of who the professor was before the semester started.

"Yeah, me too," I lie.

"Right? And Dr. Anderson is such a melodramatic name, too. I was expecting something crazy, you know? But I guess not."

I nod and smile.

"Hey, I'm gonna get back to the party," Eloise shouts. Stupid excuse to get away from me but I don't stop her. "Let's talk later, though, okay? I want to hear everything!" No she doesn't. "I miss you! You've been so busy with school and writing and stuff and I feel like I haven't seen you at all this year! Bye, Henri!"

She bounces off, blonde hair curling after her every movement, and leaps into the arms of a boy I haven't seen in my life. How on earth does she know so many people?

I'm all alone in this loud, shaking room without any friends. It's too dark to see out the windows so the flashing lights reflect off them instead, making the blues and reds even brighter. In the center of the room people tumble around, red solo cups littered on the ground with reckless abandon.

I shove my way over to the kitchen but quickly leave again—all the chemistry geniuses have made some new drug in a lab and they're testing it, huddled around the counter and rubbing their noses. I pour myself a glass of something from a pitcher and find my way up the stairs to a more quiet section of the dorm building. A few couples lean against the walls of the hallway, buried in each other's embraces or whispering into their drinks. I ignore the catch in my throat as I wander through this floor of the dorm building, getting more annoyed by the second. Where did Theo go? And why does he know people who stand on top of tables and belt out songs that were popular ten years ago?

When it gets to be too much and too loud, I make my way up the stairs of the dorm building, finally reaching a tiny door that leads out onto the roof of the building. It's identical to the one in my dorm building.

The view is incredible. The lake stretches out beyond me, a thin line of trees and a black fence separating the shore from the dirt path that winds around campus. I know that within a couple of months the water will be frozen over and the trees will be topped with snow, but for right now I want it to stay the way it looks: glowing orange and warm yellows. I can see all the way past the lake to the river beyond it, the lights of the main cluster of buildings in Haling's Cove to the east. I squint and try to find my mother's house but it blends in with the rest.

I wonder what she's doing tonight. Maybe getting quietly drunk like she does most nights, or pretending there isn't anything wrong with her relationship with Dahlia, like she's somehow a good mother and her daughter is just going through a phase all teenagers go through at one point in their lives. Maybe she thinks this is Dahlia's rebellious streak she got from our father, or maybe she thinks this is just how Dahlia is—feisty and furious. And my mother would be proud of that. She'd be proud that she has at least one strong daughter, because the other spends her life holed up inside of dark rooms reminiscent of prehistoric caves with paper and ink and a glaring screen, sipping cheap alcohol because she is just on her way to a life of alcoholism. She's on her way to becoming her mother.

"Henri," a voice says from behind me.

I turn—it's just Theo. "Oh. Hi."

"Hey. Didn't like the party?"

When I don't respond he smiles and sits down, patting the spot behind him. I sit beside him and cross my legs, sighing quietly.

"Where'd you get that from?" I ask, nodding over to the half-empty bottle of wine he has in his hand.

He shrugs. "Where do you think?" I watch as he takes a

long drink from it and then holds it out to me. I lift it and swallow, coughing slightly.

"This is terrible."

"Yeah." He stares off into space, tilting his head to the side while shrugging sheepishly and running a hand through his sand-colored hair. It falls back to where it was and settles in front of his ears. I watch as his eyes trace the landscape, admiring the way the moonlight reflects off the green. Finally he notices and I blush and look away.

Theo sniffles and takes another sip of the wine. I know that by the time we leave it will be completely gone.

"What are you thinking about?" he asks after a while.

I smile and punch him on his shoulder lightly.

"Sorry, sorry," he says.

"I'll answer it just this once," I say. "I'm thinking about how I like that I don't need to talk all the time with you. How it's comfortable to be silent." He doesn't say anything and I laugh. "And my sister. My mother, too."

"What about them?"

I shake my head, thinking. "Everything. I don't know what to do. My sister's being pretty horrible to my mother and my mom is kind of just denying it. Sometimes I don't think she even realizes what's happening."

"Why don't you say something?"

"To my mom?"

"Why not?"

I laugh again. "She doesn't understand a word I say, trust me."

"I do, but don't you think you should tell her that what

your sister is doing is wrong? And that she has the power to change it?"

"Does she, though? I don't think my mother's strong enough to confront Dahlia."

"You seriously have no faith in her?"

"If you met my mother you'd understand why."

"So...if you're not going to talk to her, what are you going to do?"

"I don't know," I say. "That's what I'm thinking about. I don't know what to do. I don't know if I *can* do anything."

"It's that bad?"

I catch his eye. "Yeah. It's pretty bad." I take the wine from him. "I guess I'll do what I always do."

"What's that?"

"Escape. Into writing, into art."

"But that doesn't do anything."

I stare at him in disbelief. "Of course it does."

His eyebrows furrow. "I don't see how reading a book or writing something will help change a very real situation that has consequences. What good are words in this kind of problem? You can't write your way out of it."

"You can write your way out of everything."

He tilts his head to the side. "Nothing I've read has ever changed my life."

"And that's why you're not a literature major."

He frowns. "Still. I don't understand it. Art isn't the end-all-be-all, you know? It can't solve real world problems."

"And computer science can?"

"Well, no, but that's not my point."

"I've gotten this far with being dependent on art."

"Art is superficial."

"Sometimes you're so naïve," I laugh. "Art isn't superficial. It's the exact *opposite*. It's everything *we* are."

"It's just pretty. You can't change anything with beauty."

Our eyes meet over the bottle of wine. I smile crookedly. "What's the purpose of beauty if it can't protect you from pain?"

He pauses and then groans. "I can't believe you've led me into a highly philosophical conversation. I'm done. No philosophy for me."

I laugh and lean against him. He spins the wine bottle in his hands, carefully examining the label like it's the first time he's seen it.

"It's supposed to rain again tomorrow," he says. "For the rest of the week, too."

"Yeah. Perfect writing weather."

"Hm. You're just going to sit inside all day?"

"Basically."

He gives me a sideways look with a tilt of his head. I want to berate him because I know he's just going to do the same thing, just playing video games instead of writing. But I keep my mouth shut and stare out at the lake, watching the little blobs that are people mill around on the beach. It must be freezing down there, this late at night.

"Hey, Henri?" Theo says. I pull my eyes away and look at him. "I... Can I kiss you?"

My mouth opens and closes again—I feel like a fish. I know I'm staring at him with my eyes wide but he doesn't seem to care. Without saying a word, my head moves on its own accord and nods.

When his fingers brush lightly over my lips I feel like I'm inside of a book, because this kind of thing doesn't happen to me normally. I almost push Theo back to explain myself: the movies I see in the wallpaper at the café, the voices that started after elementary school, the empty hole my mother left in me after recoiling into a life numbed by alcohol. I want to tell him I'm not easy—I *won't* be easy—but at the moment all I can think of is the lemony smell of his hair and the way his glasses are pushing against my forehead.

He pulls away, a small, embarrassed smile on his lips and concerned eyes boring into me. "Was that okay?"

"Yeah," I say. "Yeah, that was okay."

Instead of the normal setup of the English class where all of the seats are facing the front chalkboard, Dr. O'Kelly has rearranged the desks into a circle in the middle of the room. As people trickle in we warily take a seat, giving confused glances to each other. I pull out my notebook and a pen.

Dr. O'Kelly walks in soon, setting a tall stack of books down on his desk before sitting in one of the chairs in the circle.

"Good afternoon," he says. "I know we've been talking a lot about assigned reading and some of you complained about all of the work." He gives a look to a group of boys, who laugh and slide down in their seats. "But because this is a creative writing class, I'm well aware that all of you are working on your own creative pieces. So, instead of discussing outside literature, we're going to be discussing the literature we, in this circle, are writing."

I shift uncomfortably in my seat as the rest of the students mumble nervously to each other.

"Oh, don't worry," Dr. O'Kelly says, "it's not a test. You're in a safe environment to be vulnerable. I want to hear what you're writing about because I'm genuinely curious. I want us to go around and share the theme of something we're currently working on."

He looks at a boy wearing a pair of slacks and a button up shirt. The boy clears his throat and talks in a shaky voice.

"I'm, um, writing a play. You know. Like...about, uh, love. Kind of? Different kinds of love. Like, family, platonic, um...romantic. And stuff."

Dr. O'Kelly nods. "What about love?"

"Well, just about it. You know?"

"I'm afraid I don't." The class laughs and the boy shrinks down. "Now, I'm not saying that to embarrass you. But I don't understand—what are you trying to say about love? What is the goal? What are you trying to accomplish with your writing?"

"But—but you just asked for the theme. Mine is love."

"Yes, but 'love' is simply a theme *topic*. It's too broad to really gauge understanding. Is the theme how love corrupts? How it can alter political laws and social movements?"

"It's...I don't know. How it...how it affects the world."

"Good," he says. "That's better. We're going to work on narrowing that down a little more."

The boy gives a slight nod, face bright red. Our professor's eyes turn to the girl sitting next to him. I anxiously gaze down the line: after her, there are only two more people and then it'll be my turn. I adjust in my seat again, pulling at a loose string in the sleeve of my sweater.

The girl finishes quickly—she's clearly the type of person who has pages of research and outlines finished before she even puts down a single word of her novel. Her theme is polished, simple, and succinct, and she speaks to the professor with an airy but controlled voice.

After she finishes, the next two boys are pretty quick. They dismiss Dr. O'Kelly's suggestions with a roll of their eyes. In an instant I know they're going to end up in publishing, in one of the Big Four offices with glass windows while wearing a suit to work every day with slicked-back hair. They'll tell themselves they're going to publish, they just need to find the time to actually sit down and write their genius novels. They'll each have affairs because their perfect American wives will never satisfy them; they'll come home to steak and mashed potatoes and wine each night and return to work with bile rising in their throats.

Dr. O'Kelly turns to me. I snap out of my head and clear my throat, my hands already starting to get sweaty.

"Insanity and guilt," I say.

"Insanity *because* of guilt?"

"No. Just insanity and guilt."

He makes a note on the sheet of paper he has in front of him. My face darkens—does he think I don't understand my own work?

"We'll also need to narrow that one down a little," he says. "Both are such broad topics. And so complex."

"Yes," I say. "I'm still on the first draft, though."

He smiles politely. "Of course. I understand you're probably just getting the feel of the story, exploring the world and its characters. But, again, I think it's always best to start writing with a clear idea of where you want the story to go. Have you outlined?"

"Oh. Not...not really. I don't outline."

"May I ask why?"

"I just never have. I feel like it takes away my creative freedom, kind of. It boxes me in. I don't want to be constrained."

"I understand."

I watch as his eyes move to the next person and I let out a shaky breath. As he talks, his hands wander aimlessly and his eyebrows crease together. His skin is just starting to wrinkle, shiny with a coat of sweat, and his teeth are so white they almost look fake. The hair on the top of his head is balding and I think of birds suddenly.

I want to tell him he's a bit of an idiot.

Sometimes I hate being taller than the average 19-year-old female, but it comes in handy when I'm in bookstores. I'm able to grab books from the tallest shelves and put them back up without asking anyone for help. That's really the part I like the most: being able to help myself so I don't have to talk to anyone.

The people who work there are eager to talk, something I hate them for because aren't bookworms supposed to be shy? But I come here often enough for them to know to stay away from me.

I roam the Jane Austen shelves, wondering what book Theo would like. *Pride and Prejudice*, maybe? No. He probably read it already; you can't consider yourself an authentic Jane

Austen fan if you haven't read it. But what kinds of books does he like to read?

Sliding a few more books onto the stack I have in my hands, I make my way to the register and pay—fifty dollars, which means I'll be eating Ramen for dinner this month.

The door rings when I step outside and I grimace when I see that it has started raining. I of course don't have an umbrella, so I rearrange my coat over my head with the books tucked under my arm and race across the street to campus.

Nobody is outside. I duck under trees until I reach my dorm building, then sprint up the stairs and unlock the door to my dorm room. Clary's writing on the couch, making circles with her hands as she lays upside down.

"All the blood's going to rush to your head," I say. "You might want to get up."

"No," she responds. "I'm trying to get the blood flowing. Get some new ideas. What would a modern Julius Caesar say while getting murdered?"

" 'Don't you fucking *dare* post about this?' "

She groans.

I toss a blanket over to her and disappear into my room, setting the books down on my bed. My phone is on the desk and I dial in Theo's number.

"Hey."

"Hi, so I was just at the bookstore and I realized that I don't know what kind of books you like to read. So, tell me. I want to buy you books."

"Hang on, why were you at a bookstore so late?"

"I finished all the books I want to read here and I needed more."

"So you just drain your bank account whenever you feel like it?"

"Kind of. Who's your favorite author?"

"Jane Austen, I guess."

"I thought so. You've read *Pride and Prejudice*, right?"

"Of course I have. You don't go to libraries?"

"No, I prefer to buy every book I've ever read. I know it's more detrimental to me than helpful, but I like to be able to look back on books to see if their meanings change for me or if I find new details. It's kind of like a treasure hunt, and you can't have the same experience with books from the library."

"What are you doing for dinner tonight?"

"Probably just Ramen. Have you read anything by Virginia Woolf?"

"Yeah, but I didn't really like her writing style. Can I take you out for dinner?"

"I'm busy. I have ten books to read. What did you not like about her writing?"

"Henri," he says. "I'll answer all your questions if I can take you out to dinner."

"Dinner? Where?"

I can almost hear him shrug over the phone. "I don't know. McDonald's?"

"You sure know how to treat a person."

He laughs. "Nothing else around here is open."

"It's a fifteen minute drive," I remind him. "And I have an early class tomorrow."

"Sure you do. Come on, I'll drive in my car. We won't be gone long. Fast food is always fast. After we finish I'll take you right back to your dorm so you can go to bed. Deal?"

I sigh. "Fine."

He has an old car, one of those 80s-looking Mercedes with rust on the side mirrors and chipping beige paint. The seats, of course, are all coffee-stained and cigarette butts dot the ground. I spot at least a dozen books in the backseat. It's very Theo.

The drive is quiet and dark; I spend most of it watching the trees race by as we wind along the one-way road out of Haling's Cove, dust illuminated in the headlights. Theo switches on the radio to some annoying pop song. I quickly switch it off.

By the time we get to the McDonald's in the next town over it's pouring outside. Theo's just wearing a T-shirt and jeans so I sacrifice my sweater and race to the door, grinning back at Theo. The restaurant is practically empty except for a few obviously stoned teenagers and the workers, who all look like they just want to go home. Soaking wet with squeaking shoes, I make my way up to the counter and order two burgers with fries.

The bright fluorescent lights burn my eyes. But the order is ready soon enough and I sprint back out to the car, making sure to flick some rainwater onto Theo when I drop into the seat.

"Hey," he says, taking off his glasses to wipe the water off. "What was that for?"

I shrug. "Where are we going now?"

He smiles and starts the car, pulling out of the parking lot and driving deeper into the trees. I start to take the french fries out of the greasy bag one of the workers handed to me, but Theo puts a hand on the bag, gripping it shut, and grins wildly.

"Just wait," he says. "I promise it'll be worth it."

I start to complain and push his hands off. He laughs again.

By the time Theo stops and parks the car it has stopped raining. He tells me to wait as he gets out and wipes down the hood of the car with a towel from the trunk, tossing it into the backseat when he's finished. Then he motions me out. I roll my eyes and take the bag with me, sneaking a fry.

Theo hops onto the hood of the car.

"What on earth are you doing?" I ask.

"Come on." He pats the spot beside him. "Why did you think I was drying off the car?"

"For fun? I don't know."

He shakes his head. "Come on."

I take his hand and he pulls me up while simultaneously taking the bag from me. He sets it on his lap and pulls out the two burgers and fries, spreading a napkin between us.

"Look," he says, pointing up to the sky, "normally, if it wasn't so cloudy, you could see Saturn from here."

"Since when do you know about astronomy?" I ask him as I shove the burger into my mouth.

"I'm taking it this year," he says. "With some of my friends. But Saturn would've been right above us, over there, kind of."

I almost spit out a french fry that's drowned in salt. "Jesus, they really need to learn when to let up on the salt."

"That's the thing I never understood about McDonald's." He waves a fry in the air and I watch as it falls over limply. "Why are their fries so soggy? I mean, it's not even that hard to make regular french fries. They're always too soggy, but other fast food places have french fries that are way too crunchy."

"Like potato chips, right?"

"Exactly! They're french fries, not chips."

"I feel like McDonald's workers maybe aren't focused on making perfect french fries."

"Yeah. At least we have a McDonald's nearby. My dad used to take us here all the time, when my mom worked late and neither of them wanted to make dinner."

"What does your mom do?"

"She was a couples therapist. Ironic, really, considering how her marriage turned out."

"And your dad? What does he do?"

"He was a plumber. He hated it, though. My mom was always trying to get him to switch jobs, even to something that paid less, but he was the most stubborn person ever. He said he wanted to finish what he'd started."

"What's he doing now?"

"He died."

"Oh. I'm sorry, Henri. I didn't know."

"It's okay." I finish my burger and crunch the paper in my hands, placing it back in the bag. "They divorced two months before he was diagnosed. Cancer, in his lungs. He used to smoke so many cigarettes when I was little. And he wouldn't even pick up the butts, he'd just leave them lying around the house for Dahlia to come and put in her mouth."

"Did she ever choke?"

"No. She was too smart for that. After a few times of

swallowing the butts she'd just spit them back out because they tasted so terrible."

"I bet."

"The worst part was that my mom wouldn't let us go visit him in the hospital. I had to skip classes to go see him."

"What? Why wouldn't she let you?"

I shrug. "I don't know. They got kind of competitive with each other after he left. They would always give Dahlia and me loads of money whenever we asked for it. I actually still have a lot of it left because I never really spent it. I guess they were both trying to be the favorite parent."

He's quiet and I know I've just said something he doesn't know how to respond to. I immediately feel bad, and scold myself for even bringing something like this up.

"It's okay now," I say. "I mean, Dahlia isn't acting great, but I still go over to my mom's house. For a while I wouldn't talk to her."

"Dahlia's still being lame?"

"Yeah."

"That sucks. I'm sorry, Henri."

"Don't apologize, you didn't do anything. And it's not like there's anything I can do about it."

"Why not?"

"Because she's my sister. I can't just go and berate her."

"Henri, you can't just not do anything."

"Then what exactly am I supposed to do? Am I supposed to be a terrible person and accuse my sister of abuse? Or am I supposed to be a bystander and just watch it happen right in front of me?"

"I think...I think you need to help your mother, Henri. It's not going to end well. I said this earlier, I know." He takes a breath and looks back up to the sky. "But I don't think you'd be able to live with yourself if you didn't do anything. Right? Wouldn't you feel so guilty?"

"Yeah, probably. It just feels wrong. To say something like that, about my sister."

"I understand," he says. "Actually, no, I don't. I'm not in your situation. But I really think you need to talk to your mother, or at least some professional who can actually do something."

"What, like a therapist?"

"Maybe."

I laugh. "Yeah, right. I don't think that would solve anything."

He gives me a look. "Are you just saying that because of your mom?"

"No. I seriously don't think it would help. Dahlia...she's insatiable. She takes everything from my mom because in her mind my mom took everything from her. It's stupid, kind of."

"I don't think so. I think that's a pretty normal reaction for an immature teenager to have."

"I guess." I pull my legs to my chest and rest my chin on my knees. "Sometimes I hate her. Sometimes I absolutely hate her so much it's hard not to grab her by the shoulders and shake her until she gets dizzy. I want to scream at her and tell her she's a terrible person because of what she's doing to our mother. I want to tell her that it's not a game, that she's a person, and you can't treat someone like that."

"Then tell her that."

"I can't. She's my little sister. If I said something like that to her..." I pause and turn my head to look in Theo's direction. "Wouldn't *I* be a horrible person, then?"

"No," he says simply. "I think you'd just be a person."

"Hello?" I call after knocking on the door of my mom's house. "Is anyone home?"

I slip off my jacket and head into the kitchen, where I see Dahlia pulling a warm pizza out from the oven. She's wearing pajama pants and a loose tank top, her hair in a tight bun at the nape of her neck. She looks up, placing the pan on the top of the stove, and sees me in the doorway.

"Oh, hey," she says.

"What are you doing?" I ask while untying my shoes.

"Making pizza. Mom and I are watching a movie together."

I pause. "What?"

"Yeah. Could you get the cookies from the shelf behind you? I want to make a little platter for us. You can watch the movie with us, too, if you want."

"Oh." I run a hand through my hair and turn to the shelf, finding a small container of day-old chocolate chip cookies. I hand them to Dahlia and sit on a stool as she cuts into the warm pizza. "Yeah, sure."

She doesn't really acknowledge my response, just finds three glasses and fills them with water, nodding over to them.

"Could you give one of those to Mom, and tell her I'll be back soon?"

"Yeah."

I balance them in my hands and walk over to the living room, where my mother is curled up on the couch underneath a plaid blanket.

"Hey, Mom," I say, setting the water on the coffee table and sinking down next to her, slightly concerned.

"Henri! I didn't know you were coming."

"Yeah, I didn't either. I just needed a break from school."

She takes a sip of her water and nods her head.

"Um," I say. "So, you're watching a movie? With Dahlia?"

"Yes, she came home from school and since she has no homework tonight I figured it was fine if we watched something together. She asked to spend some time with me."

"She wanted to hang out with you?"

She smiles. "Yes. Is that such a surprise?"

I want to say yes, but I shake my head vigorously. "No, of course not. She's just normally with her friends all the time. I didn't think that..."

"Dinner's ready!" Dahlia says.

I jump up to help her carry the pizza and cookies inside. She laughs and we sit down together, me in between the two of them. Dahlia settles under another blanket and I curl my legs underneath myself as she presses play.

"I've wanted to see this for forever," Dahlia says, grinning at me.

I look and smile just like the columns inside the Hagia Sophia—visually contradicting the burden they (and I) must carry.

Halfway through, I say I have to go to the bathroom and retreat back to my old bedroom, where I pull out my phone and call Theo. He picks up immediately.

"Hey," he says.

"Hi. Could we meet at the bookstore in ten minutes?"

"Sure. Is something wrong?"

"No. Well, maybe. I'm not really sure. I just need to talk to someone."

His tone shifts and I can hear him become worried. "Okay. Yeah, I'll leave right now."

"Okay. Thank you, Theo."

"Yeah. See you soon."

He hangs up and I leave my room, walking back out to the living room. I pause when I see my mom and Dahlia together on the couch. It seems so unnatural.

I step forward and lay a hand on my mom's shoulder. She looks up.

"I have to go," I tell her. "I forgot that I'm meeting someone at the bookstore."

"Oh, sure," she says. "Have fun. Thank you for coming."

"Yeah," I say. "Bye."

"Bye!"

I grab my jacket and slide on my shoes, leaving before Dahlia can rise from the couch and say whatever she was going to say to me.

Outside is cold. The sharpness of the air surprises me and I close the door behind me, stuffing my hands into my pockets before starting off down the road to town. My breath comes out in white puffs, disappearing just as I notice them. It's hard for me to put one foot in front of the other; I am not dressed for this weather. Still, I walk on. I just need to talk to Theo.

He's already at the bookstore, waiting outside with his arms crossed and a beanie pulled low over his ears. He sees me and starts forward, a concerned look on his face. We meet each other and pause in the middle of the sidewalk.

"Are you okay?" he asks.

"Yeah. I think so. Can we go inside first? I'm freezing."

He nods and opens the door for me, waiting to go in until I do. My hands immediately warm the second I step inside, and I pull off my jacket and scarf. Theo rubs his hands together, taking off his layers as well, and we begin to move around the bookstore slowly.

"Where were you?" he asks quietly.

"My mom's house."

"Oh," he says flatly. "Did anything happen? With Dahlia?"

"No, not really. That was why I was kind of freaked out." I look up at him. "This is going to sound stupid now, but it seemed really normal. When I walked in Dahlia was making dinner for the two of them because they were going to watch a movie. Together. Which never happens. I didn't want to say anything to either of them, but the whole thing just felt so strange."

"You mean because Dahlia was being normal?"

"I guess. I know this is weird, and it's probably nothing. I'm just not really used to seeing Dahlia wanting to hang out with my mom. On a school night especially. I don't understand. The last time I was there with both of them, Dahlia was terrible to her, and now she's being so nice. I don't know what happened."

"I don't know either."

I sigh. "Yeah. I think I maybe just need to get my mind off of it."

"Right. Well, can I make a deal with you?"

I give him a look. "Depends."

"If you can guess how many books I've read this week, I'll buy you two books."

I laugh. "What? Seriously?"

"Sure."

"Theo, the books here are pretty expensive."

He shrugs. "It's fine."

"No, I'm serious. Just one, okay?"

"Henri—"

"I'll only take one."

He sighs. "Fine."

"Okay. This week?"

He nods, his grin widening.

"Um...well, it's been pretty rainy all week. You haven't been able to go outside that much. But you might've also been playing video games while you're inside."

"True," he concedes.

"So...my guess is two."

"Two books?"

"Yeah."

I look at him expectantly and he shakes his head with a smile on his face.

"Sadly, no. I've read three."

I groan and push him backwards. "So unfair. But we can still look at all the pretty books."

He nods and we walk along the shelves, mostly quiet, but sometimes I find a book I think he'd like and point it out to him. He makes a note of the title on his phone and then we move on to the next shelf.

Finally, we come to my favorite section of the store: the classics. They're all bound in cloth or leather, so I run a hand along their spines.

"Is this a habit of yours?" he asks amusedly.

I roll my eyes. "Don't tell me you don't like the feel of leather-bound books."

"I mean, I do, but it's not like I want to touch every single one of them I see."

"Fine. I'm weird."

"Definitely."

"I might have a bit of a soft spot for leather-bound books. Even if I have a copy of the book, I'll still sometimes buy another version of it just because I like the way it looks."

"What book do you have the most copies of?"

I smile. "*The Bell Jar.*"

"Oh, gosh. How many copies?"

I grin devilishly and turn to face him. "Ten."

"*Ten?* How is that even possible? They actually have ten versions of the book?"

"You'd be surprised at what you can find at thrift stores and indie bookstores."

"How do you have space for all of them?"

"I keep most of them at my house," I say, shrugging. "My mom doesn't really mind the piles of books in my room."

"You're so weird."

"Look at this one," I say, pointing to a copy of *Wuthering Heights.* "See? Who wouldn't want that on their bookshelf?"

"Do you want it?" Theo asks me.

"Of course I do. But I'm currently broke and spending my money on this probably isn't the best idea."

He grabs the book from the shelf and tucks it underneath his arm, pulling me to the entrance of the store, where a worker is seated behind a cash register. Theo places the book on the table and takes out a debit card.

"Theo," I say, "no. I guessed wrong."

He smiles at me. "That doesn't mean I don't want to buy you a book."

I know I shouldn't be up right now, because it's still dark outside. I groan and roll over into my pillow, running a hand through my knotty hair. It's cold and I don't want to get out of bed.

Clary's banging around in the kitchen, making loud noises with pots and pans as if she's deliberately trying to annoy me. My eyes close for a moment and then snap back open: why is she up so early? She's definitely not a morning person.

I turn over and read my alarm clock. Four in the morning.

"Clary?" I call as I get out of bed. "Is that you? What on earth are you doing up so early?" I pull on a wool sweater strewn on the ground and open the door, pausing when I see who it is. "Go away, Dad."

He looks over his shoulder at me, hands hovering over the pan of eggs he's cooking. A smile spreads over his waxy face.

"Henri, hey. I was wondering when you'd wake up. You snore a lot, you know that?"

I sigh. "Yeah, I know." Quietly, in case Clary does happen to be here and is asleep, I walk over to the kitchen and pour myself a bowl of cereal from the cupboard, making sure not to make contact with my father. I grab a spoon and sit at the table.

The eggs crackle in the pan and he throws handfuls of spinach and salt onto them. I watch as he makes his way over to the fridge and grabs what I knew he would: ketchup. He returns to the stovetop, squirts on some of the sauce, turns off the burner, and comes to sit across from me with the still-hot pan in his hands. He sets it down on the table with a muffled *clang*. I spoon the dry cereal into my mouth.

"How's school?" he asks.

I shrug. "Fine."

"Are your classes as useless as I said they would be?"

"No. They're interesting."

"How's your mother?"

"Like you care."

"I do." He frowns at me and takes a bite of his eggs. "How are things with Clary and Eloise?"

"Fine, all fine, Dad. I don't want to talk about this right now."

"Then what do you want to talk about?"

"Nothing. I want you to leave."

He smiles. "No you don't, Henri."

He's right and he knows it. Still, that doesn't make me any less angry with this sudden arrival. I want him to go because I can't focus with him here, but I want him to stay because I know if I send him away I might never see him again.

"I met a boy," I find myself saying. "His name's Theo."

"Ah. What does he study?"

"Computer science." My dad makes a face and I scoff at him. "What's wrong with that?"

"Never thought you'd like the science nerds."

"I like this one. The others are insufferable, but he's okay."

"Hm. I hope he knows how to keep a conversation, because you sure don't."

"Rude, Dad."

"It's true. How is your mother, Henri? I want to know."

"She's fine."

"The truth. I want to know the truth."

I slam my spoon into my bowl and jump at how loud it is. Anxiously, I look to Clary's door, but the light doesn't turn on and I don't hear a sound from inside. I shouldn't really be worried—she could sleep through an earthquake if she wanted to.

"Why are you here, Dad? I said I don't want to talk to you, *especially* about Mom. She's doing fine. Dahlia is fine. I'm fine, we're all fine. You don't need to be here bothering me, okay? We're all one big, happy family like we always have been since you left."

He's quiet for a moment before leaning forward and raising his eyebrows. "I don't believe you."

"I don't really care what you believe. You're an asshole and I hope you know it."

"You can't blame me for dying."

"No, but I *can* blame you for ruining our lives."

He sits back in his chair and looks at me. "You don't understand, Henri. You were too young to understand. If I'd stayed, that house would have been destroyed. Your mother and I were never going to work out. No matter what we did, no matter how much therapy we paid for, nothing would have brought us back together. We would have taken you both down in the process of tearing each other apart."

"You don't get to say that," I spit. "You don't get to blame this on your hatred for each other. You're not right. If you loved each other once you could have again. You *didn't* hate each other."

"Henri—"

"No! No, you didn't hate each other, because how else do you explain this? How else do you explain Mom drinking herself to sleep every night since you left? How do you explain Dahlia acting out like this, and me being this idiotic failure? If you'd hated each other Mom would have hated both of us. And she didn't, Dad. She loved us. She loved us so much she ruined us."

He shakes his head. "She hated *me* so much she ruined you two."

"You're not listening to me. Mom told me to go live out my dream here. She told me I could be this great, published, world-famous author and look at me now. I've never finished a story in my life. I barely understand the book I'm writing. My professor can even see I'm not meant to be a writer, because I don't understand the stupid *theme* of my novel."

He shakes his head. "I told you so, Henri. I told you this degree wouldn't help you."

"Don't say that. That's not true. And Dahlia, look at Dahlia. How can you say hatred shaped her? She attacks Mom with every chance she gets because she wants to prove she's some kind of martyr, some kind of strong hero who doesn't need love. And I wonder who taught her that."

"I never said I didn't love you."

"You didn't show it."

"I can't right my wrongs, I know that, Henri. But you have to understand that I did love you and Dahlia. Otherwise I wouldn't have left. I did what was best. I did what I thought would help you two, even if it meant removing myself from your lives."

"You really think you're that terrible of a person?"

"I do. And you do too."

"I don't think you're a terrible person. I just think you're stupid."

He smiles sadly, the wrinkles on the edges of his eyes tilting upwards. "I know you think I'm terrible. I know, because you see yourself in me and hate that you do."

"You don't even know me."

"But I do. I know you because I *am* you."

It's a man, she sees. A man at the door wearing the same clothes her husband wore every day to work. He has the same look in his eyes, the one her husband gave her when he was scared: that dark, vaguely threatening stare that makes her skin crawl and feel like she's about to shrivel back up into herself. She shivers and ignores the way her still-wet summer dress scratches her calves as she walks toward him.

"I told you," she says. "I told you I don't want to see you again. You know that Adelaide—"

"I don't care about Adelaide," the man says, "I don't care if she knows."

"She would hate me. Even more than she does now."

"Then does it really matter? She'll hate either way."

She grimaces and recoils further into the house. She offers tea, coffee, water, anything to show the man she's just being a good hostess. Just a hostess, she tells herself. Because she regrets their weekend getaways when she told her husband she had planned a trip with her friends, she regrets the bottles of wine she rediscovered in the garbage cans of their shared hotel rooms, she regrets missing this man and turning away from her husband in favor of him.

"I can't," she says again. "I made a choice, and I chose my husband."

The man scoffs. "He's dead."

This makes her angry. "Yes, he's dead. Of course I know that. But I wasn't faithful during his life. I can at least be faithful during his death."

"You're an idiot. A raving, obsessive idiot, you know that? You threw yourself at me, you said you were tired and bored of him and needed to get away. You said he wouldn't listen to you, you said you needed a change. And now you'll leave just because he died and you feel bad? You remember how he treated you. He wasn't a good husband—not even death can change that. His death does not change anything."

"But it does," she says. Quietly, as if she's starting to make a snack for the two of them, she opens a kitchen drawer and pulls out a knife. She lays it on the counter and turns her back on the man to get some carrots and bell peppers and cucumbers from the fridge. He sits down heavily on the couch, then gets back up and leans on the counter opposite of her, watching as she washes the vegetables and sets them on a cutting board to slice up.

"You don't understand," she says. "I feel guilty now. I should have felt it earlier, when we still had time, but I can't change it now."

"That's stupid," the man says. "That's the stupidest thing I've ever heard. Aren't you free? You told me you hated him. Isn't this your chance to live again?"

"You make it sound like I was in jail."

"You were."

"Don't be so dramatic."

She finishes chopping up the vegetables and scrapes them into a green plastic bowl, setting the knife back down on the counter and resisting the urge to run a finger along the edge. He stares at her as she moves around the kitchen and gathers ingredients for the salad she wants to make.

"Don't do that," he says. "Come on."

She looks up at him, confused. "What?"

"I know what you're doing. You weren't a housewife, you weren't a good wife. You didn't make healthy salad or nice meals for him because you didn't care about him. Stop trying to play this role, this person you aren't."

"I don't know what you're talking about."

"Of course you do! This guilting me into whatever you want isn't going to work, okay? I'm not buying it."

"Buying what?"

"Stop trying to pretend like you're a wife in mourning. I know you don't care. I know you're practically relieved he's dead."

"Don't say that. Don't say that to me."

"I'll say whatever I want to you."

She slams the bowl down on the counter but the gesture looks more pathetic than angry. Heaving, she points towards the door.

"Get out. Get out right now."

He shakes his head. "You know I'm right. You know I'm right and you're scared, aren't you? You're so scared."

"I'm not scared. Not of you and not of how I feel. I loved my husband. I loved him because he loved me and he loved our daughter. You don't get to tell me how I felt about him. Yes, I regret cheating on him with a man like you. I regret cheating on him with you. But I couldn't tell him that while he was alive, so I'm going to tell him that while he's dead. And I want you to leave, right now."

"You'll never stop the guilt. This won't solve anything."

"Maybe not," she says, "but it'll help ease the pain."

"My god, you're so naïve."

"I swear, get out right now."

"Are you even listening to yourself? Your husband is dead. Got it? He can't come back to berate you or to love you. You're here, I'm here. He's not."

"Get out. I'm not going to say it again."

"You're pitiful."

"Get. Out."

He laughs suddenly, sharp and painful. Adelaide's mother straightens her posture as he stands and leans his hands on the counter, coming closer to her.

"No," he says.

Her hands move too fast for her to realize what she's doing. One grips the hilt of the knife she used to cut vegetables, the other tightens around the collar of his shirt. His eyes bulge and she watches in delight, wondering what it would feel like to see the knife slice through him. She can imagine the blood coating her hands and wrists—velvety and thick—and the smell of iron. She wants to see him fall face down on her kitchen counter, his blood the dressing to the salad he made fun of. She wants to see his mouth open and close like a blubbering fish and his teeth stain deep red. She wants to see his eyes widen even more and slowly close, her always in the peripheral.

And because she has always been a person who chases after her dreams, she kills him.

Clary calls from the kitchen, repeating herself when I don't answer. I groan and pull the covers over my head.

"Henri," she shouts. "Do you want anything for breakfast? I'm making pancakes."

My door opens and a stream of bright light floods in. I grimace and burrow further into my bed, silently cursing her in my head.

"Henri," Clary says again. "Do you want food? Hello?"

"No, I'm not hungry," I snap.

"Okay..." She turns to leave and then looks back at me, frowning. "You're not sick, are you? Because you know I have to go to that show later this week, and I can't be sick on opening night."

"I *know*. I'm sick, just leave me alone."

She fake-gasps and shuts the door, rushing back into the kitchen. I hear her banging pots and pans around again and think of my dad yesterday morning. That only makes me feel worse.

Slowly, I swing my legs out of bed and take the blankets with me, around my shoulders like a cape, and grab my computer from my desk, returning back to my bed. I open it, eyes squinting in the blue light, and log in.

For a while I just sit there, staring at the screen. I don't feel like writing, not right now, and even watching TV seems like too much work.

My thoughts drift—to school and the classes I'm missing, to Theo, to my mother and to Dahlia. I remind myself of what's probably happening in the house right now. I can almost see it: Dahlia shouting at my mother while she cowers in a corner, like some kind of stray puppy. A wave of hatred washes over me but I catch myself.

I close the computer and set it on my bedside table. The room is dark and peaceful again, even though it's mid-afternoon. I look over at the blackout curtains, suddenly glad

I bought them over the summer. Yawning, I roll over and fall asleep again.

Adelaide's trek over campus to her class is sluggish. When she gets there, the lecture hall is already full and she slides into a seat near the back, wishing she were anywhere but here. She sees a few of her friends in the front rows—always overachievers, of course— but ignores them when they look back and see her, calling her name. She can't deal with them today.

The professor clears his throat and claps his hands. He pulls his trousers up in a comical sort of way and while the rest of the class laughs, Adelaide is imagining the bathroom: specifically, the pills in her mother's medicine cabinet.

When her professor starts to talk she decides what she's going to do. She stands and quietly leaves the hall, shivering at the gusts of wind outside. Her pace picks up into a jog and she runs all the way to her mother's house in town. There aren't any people on the streets and her mother's car isn't in the driveway. She lets out a shaky breath.

The door is unlocked but it doesn't bother Adelaide. She's used to her mother being forgetful.

She steps into the foyer and her nose crinkles. It smells like bleach and peppermint soap. Sliding off her shoes, she looks around the corner, calling for her mother. No one answers.

Before she heads to the bathroom she opens the fridge and finds a vegetable salad. She scoffs and pours it into the trash just to annoy her mother.

The bathroom is near the back of the house and she makes sure not to look into her parents' room across the hallway. She opens the medicine cabinet and is faced with pill bottles in all the colors of the rainbow, different sizes and shapes. She blindly reaches for any, without reading the labels, and opens one, peering inside. White, round pills.

Her head snaps up as she hears the front door creak open. Someone slides their shoes off and she stuffs the pills back into the cabinet.

"Mom?"

"Yeah, I'm home," she hears.

Shit. She closes the cabinet as quietly as she can and rushes into the living room, seeing her mother standing in front of the fridge.

"Did you eat that salad I made?" she asks.

Adelaide shakes her head and slumps onto the couch. "No, I threw it out because it smelled weird. It was stinking up the whole house."

"Hm." Adelaide's mother grabs a drink from the fridge—apple juice in a plastic bottle—and comes to sit next to her daughter. "How come you're home? Are you sick?"

"No, I just forgot my favorite blanket here."

"Don't you have blankets in your dorm room?"

"Well, yeah, but not my favorite one."

"Hm." She takes a sip and holds it out to Adelaide, who shakes her head and frowns, noticing the dark brown stains on her mother's yellow dress.

"Did you spill something on your dress? It looks kind of like coffee or something."

"Yes. I made coffee this morning and wasn't paying attention. I reached into the microwave and..." She gestures to the stains.

"Why didn't you change, then? And where were you?"

"I didn't realize this would be an interrogation."

"It's not, I'm just—"

"I know, I know. Don't get offended. I was looking at grave markers. For..."

Adelaide looks away, through the window into the backyard. She feels her face heating up and lips beginning to twitch but tries as hard as she can to keep the tears from falling. She can't cry in front of her mother.

"Lots of rain," she says instead. "The campus walkways have been flooded."

"I bet. The front yard was completely covered with water. I went out and took the squash from the street. They were dirty, though. I assume the rain has washed them off."

"Yeah."

They're quiet for the next few minutes, Adelaide's mother drinking the apple juice and Adelaide suppressing the urge to shout at her because of the loud slurping noises she's making. She tries to ignore it and thinks instead about the lecture she's missing. She's glad she's not there: she would probably be ready to leap out of there right now, but being alone with her mother isn't any better. She's still agitated and fidgety and angry.

"I have to go to the grocery store," her mother announces suddenly. "I can drive you back to campus if you want."

"Oh. Yeah, sure. Thanks."

She slides off the couch and walks to her room, savoring the quiet before getting her blanket and tucking it in her arms. Her mother is in the foyer, putting on a raincoat, with the car keys jangling in her hand. They leave the house together, Adelaide one step behind her mother, and get into the car without a word. Finally, when Adelaide's mother starts the car, the rumble of the engine ruptures their awkward silence.

The entire town seems to be in mourning too. Adelaide hadn't noticed when she'd returned to college and when she'd walked back to her house earlier—her mind had been too busy. But now, she's able to look out the window like she has never seen the outside world before. All of the yellowish front lawns have a layer of water over the grass, and a few people are outside, attempting to scoop buckets of water from the yard. Adelaide almost opens the window and screams at them, because it's absolutely pointless and they look stupid. But she doesn't; instead, she clenches her fists and digs her fingernails into her palms, both cursing and thanking her mother silently.

Her mother, strangely, is quiet. Normally she'd be talking during awkward car rides, but so far she hasn't said a word to Adelaide.

Adelaide knows she didn't make coffee this morning. Her mother never drinks coffee, because she thinks it makes a person forget themself and lose control. She waves off the brown stains (they could easily be from mud) but doesn't understand why her mother would lie to her about making coffee, of all things.

"Mom," she says. Her mother gives a small grunt to acknowledge that she's listening. "I think...I think after this semester I might take a break from college."

She slams on the brakes in the middle of the road. "What?"

"I just don't think now is a good time for me to be in school. I've always wanted to take a gap year, you know that, but I think now is a good time for that. I'll come back, of course. I always do."

"No," her mother says, shaking her head. "Absolutely not. Your father dying doesn't mean you can completely ruin your life."

"It wouldn't be ruining it, Mom. I need a break. Mentally and emotionally."

"No," her mother repeats. "No. I'm paying your tuition and I say no."

"But why?"

"Because you are a student. You're not going to frolic across the globe while I stay here paying for it all. When I gave birth to you, I made a deal, alright? In that deal was paying for four years of college, not paying for a year off to waste your life."

"You wouldn't have to pay for it. I would get another job."

"No. You'll never want to go back to school."

"Maybe not, but I would anyway. Okay? I'm not stupid. I know how important getting a degree is."

"Absolutely not." She starts the car and the windows begin to fog up, either from the temperature drop outside or the angry heat emanating from the two women. "Your father would hate this. He knew how important a complete education is. I mean, you would be a year older than all of your classmates. How horrible would that be? You would hate it. Everyone would hate it. You would be that one weird student in class who spent a year of her life doing absolutely nothing. I am not going to let you be a failure. I do not raise failures."

"Jeez, Mom, it's not like I'm dropping out. People take gap years all the time."

"You would have to reapply."

"They'll take me. They understand, they know what happened."

"No. It's too expensive."

"I already said you wouldn't have to pay for it."

"Well, I can't exactly just sit here and expect you to fend for yourself."

"Yes you can. That's what would happen after college anyway."

"Yes, after you've gotten a degree and are eligible for high-paying jobs."

"Mom, it's not really your decision. I'm an adult now."

"And who pays for your tuition?"

"I don't understand why you don't want me to do this. People do it all the time."

"Adelaide, it's final. I'm paying for your school and I say no."

"I'm just going to struggle, you realize that, right? I can't pay attention in school. Lectures are boring and I just want to sleep all the time."

"Then you make yourself coffee and get to work."

"It's not that simple, Mom! I can't just kiss grief goodbye and wish it well. It's impacting my focus. I can't spend another year doing this again, okay? I will literally go crazy."

"We'll put you on medication, we'll do whatever we need to. But you are not missing a year of school because you can't cope with your father's death. That's inexcusable."

"I feel like that's a pretty good excuse for taking a gap year."

"No. I already said no, and now I'm tired of this conversation. We're almost there. I don't want to hear about this again, alright?"

The car pulls up to the school's entrance and Adelaide opens the car door in a huff, forgetting her blanket in the seat as she covers her head with a sleeve and rushes to the nearest building, shuddering as blasts of wind cross her path.

Her mother waits in the car, watching her and gripping the steering wheel so tight her knuckles turn white. She swears she could kill her daughter and almost laughs at the thought—what would happen if the police found two dead bodies in one day, both somehow connected to her?

It all comes back, she thinks as she puts the car in drive and pulls away from the campus. It all comes back to me.

Someone's knocking on my door. I groan and throw a

pillow at it, flinging an arm over my forehead as I roll over in bed. I don't want to deal with anyone right now. I've had my fill of people to last me for at least another few weeks.

"Henri," Clary whines from outside. "*Henri*. Your professor is calling."

My eyes open into slits. "Which one?" My voice is husky and sounds like gravel.

"I don't know. He didn't say, he just asked to talk to you. Said he's sorry for the early call but he wanted to talk to you before the lecture started today. Just take the phone, okay?"

I drag myself out of bed and open the door, stepping into the light with my squinty eyes, but Clary has already disappeared into her room. The phone is on the kitchen table.

Balancing it between the side of my face and my shoulder, I groggily start to make a cup of coffee for myself, grabbing a frozen pod of coffee from the freezer and running boiling water over it from the sink. I typically don't like to use these, because Clary always buys them for me despite her dislike of coffee and I know how expensive they are. But it doesn't really matter—I'm sure it doesn't seem expensive to her and her father.

"Hello?" I say into the phone.

"Henri! I was wondering how much longer you'd be. I found your dorm room's number in the school directory." It's Dr. Anderson, of course. Only he would call someone at eight in the morning. "I've noticed you've been absent from class these past few days. I was just wondering if something happened? Are you planning on coming back at all?"

"Oh," I say. "Yeah. I'm sick."

"Oh, I'm sorry. I know how horrible that can be. Well, I do

have some notes from the lectures you've missed that I think would be helpful to get a hold of. Do you have a friend in the class who can drop it off at your dorm?"

My mind wanders to Theo. "Uh, you know, I do, but I'm pretty sick and I don't want to get someone else sick. My roommate is already hiding from me. Could you just...email it to me, maybe?" I can't talk face-to-face with another human being right now. I will literally go into breakdown mode.

"Of course. Well, I hope you feel better. We're moving steadily through history. Time travelers, we are!"

"Mhm," I say. "Thanks. Bye."

I hang up and toss the phone onto the couch, where I lower myself down and take a sip of the coffee. It's bitter and tastes terrible, but I force it down my throat because I haven't eaten anything in a day and I need some sort of energy. My cell phone, in my bedroom, chimes. Dr. Anderson is punctual —not something I'd expect.

I walk into my room and grab the phone from my bed. Sure enough, there's the email: "To Henri, hope this helps!" And he uses exclamation points. How very professional of him.

I click it open and am faced with at least ten documents. I open one and scroll down. It's probably thirty pages long. I know myself well enough to understand that I'll just read over these, not actually take notes on them, so I skim over the notes from the files he sent over. They're already on early Europe. Dr. Anderson's speedy. Or maybe I've missed more class than I thought.

I start to think I should keep a journal or something. Just to keep track of what I've been doing, because that's what everyone seems to be doing now—as if half of the world's population will go extinct and they'll be this generation's Anne Frank.

But then I laugh, because what on earth would I write about? Lying in bed all day and sleeping is only so entertaining.

I can imagine the entries: *November 16—Today, I slept for 16 hours. Woke up at 3 PM and drank a cup of coffee. It tasted terrible.*

November 17—Today, I slept for 15 hours. I wanted to sleep more but for some reason I couldn't. Looked over art history papers and decided I don't need to learn more about Caravaggio. He was a jerk anyway.

November 18—Today, I slept for 14 hours. Theo still hasn't called.

November 19—Today, I slept for 11 hours. Clary begged me to clean up my room because it was starting to smell. While she was in class I put my dirty dishes in the sink for her to wash and I piled my dirty clothes into my closet. Hopefully she won't smell them.

November 20—Today, I slept for 19 hours. Mom called and I ignored the phone for the first time ever.

November 21—Today, I slept for 18 hours. I tried to write a paper for my English poetry class but gave up after the first sentence. I don't think poetry is really my thing anyway.

November 22—Today, I slept for 20 hours. It was a good day. Except for the email I got from one of the school counselors. I ignored it for a while, then responded to tell them I just had a bad case of the flu and hoped it would be over soon.

November 23—Today, I slept for 9 hours. Clary was being loud because she had friends over. Sometimes I hate her so much and I just want to scream at her to shut up. Sometimes I wish this entire building would collapse.

November 24—Today, I slept for 17 hours. I ate stale waffles straight from the freezer and got a brain freeze. It felt sort of nice, in a way.

I decide maybe I won't start a journal.

Adelaide is in her dorm room, sitting on her bed, staring at a letter that she wishes she'd never received. Her first reaction is to laugh and accuse Archie of seeing things. After all, he's nearing eighty years old and his eyesight can't be trusted. Right?

That's what she wants to tell herself, but she knows him too well to convince herself of that. He's never wrong, and if he says he saw what he wrote in this letter, then he definitely saw it.

She could scream. She might have screamed, if it wasn't exam season and the student next door wasn't studying for an exam the next day. She settles for smashing her head between her palms and kicking her mattress again and again.

Aside from screaming, she could also kill her mother.

Adelaide looks back at the letter and her eyes catch on certain phrases: 'blue, four-wheeled pickup truck that pulled up nearly on top of the curb'; 'a man wearing a dark navy blue jumpsuit with "Bill" embroidered on his left breast pocket'; 'door opening quickly'; 'silence after'; 'the recycling bins always rattled with the sound of glass whenever your father brought out the trash—but I know he didn't like to drink, and I know your mother respected that, so I wondered: who else was drinking in that house?'; 'I don't think she realized she wasn't being careful enough, but maybe I'm just too nosey'; 'I regret to be the one to tell you, but I think that your mother and this man, "Bill," might have been having an—'

She folds the letter over itself again, pressing it down into the blanket. Her mouth is dry—is it always this dry? She can feel her heart beating inside of her ribcage, like some kind of crazed bird that will tear its way out.

Then the thought arrives: she has to talk to her mother. No, she has to question, to confront, to pressure her mother into telling her the truth. Because she can't simply walk up to her and ask about something like this, because it will completely change everything she ever knew about her mother and her father and their marriage. It will completely change everything about her life.

She stands with a start, grabbing a jacket from her desk chair and pulling her arms through it. Without thinking about what she'll say to her mother, how she'll approach the topic, she locks the door to her dorm room and walks off campus.

Her sneakers are going to be soaked, she knows—there's a layer of at least one inch of water covering the pathways. The grass is flooded and she briefly wonders how exactly ants survive these kinds of floods. Do they float, or swim? Can they even swim? Their arms (legs?) certainly aren't big enough to push themselves forward, she thinks. So do they just drown? She almost laughs as she imagines it: small groups of ants, flitting around in the water and twirling down like a whirlpool. Maybe they're gasping for air as they go. Maybe they're fighting or maybe they've accepted it. She likes to believe that, if she were an ant, she would just accept her fate and let the water carry her down. She likes to think it would be peaceful, but she knows that in reality drowning is anything but peaceful.

A knock sounds on my door. I throw a hand over my eyes and sigh. Can't Clary take a hint? I've been in bed for days, which probably means I don't want to be bothered. At all.

"What?" I say, starting to get more annoyed now that she won't just say what she wants. "Clary, I'm trying to sleep."

The door opens and a blond head peeks in. "It's not Clary."

I sit up straight, running a hand through my hair in a panic. I must look like such a mess. "Theo—uh, hi. I didn't know you were coming over. You didn't—you didn't call. You haven't called. Recently."

"Yeah, sorry about that. I just thought you might need some space."

"What? Why?"

"Well, after our last talk you seemed kind of...I don't know, kind of down. I just didn't want to bother you. I know stuff at home is difficult right now, so I just wanted to let you sort through all that without feeling like you had to talk to me so much."

"Oh," I say. "That's surprisingly thoughtful."

"Surprisingly?"

"Not in a bad way, I mean. I just...most people wouldn't be like that. So, thanks."

"Yeah. Um...well, I guess I didn't expect you to need to be alone for...this long. I mean, not that it's bad. It's fine, I get it. I just kind of missed you. Talking to you. So I thought maybe you'd want to go to the bakery, just for coffee and a croissant or something?"

"Oh. I'd normally say yes, but I'm not super...presentable right now." I force a husky laugh. "Yeah. So, thanks, but I can't."

"Henri."

"Yeah?"

"What's going on?"

I frown and pull the covers around me. "Nothing. I'm just tired and want to be alone."

"You've been tired and alone for the past two weeks."

"So?"

"So, that's a little worrying for someone who cares about you."

"I'm fine, really. You don't have to worry."

"Well, I'm worried. Can you please just come outside and eat something? You need fresh air. It's not good to stay cooped up in a dark cave all the time."

"First of all, this isn't a cave, it's my room. Secondly, why do you think you get to tell me what to do?"

"Because you're clearly not taking care of yourself, Henri, and I care about you. I don't want to see you like this. This isn't you."

"Maybe it is. How well do you really know me? We met maybe a month ago."

He shakes his head. "Please stop arguing with me. I really don't want to fight, I'm just trying to help you. Please let me buy you coffee."

I stare at him, face reddening in the dark. I want to ask him if Clary put him up to this just to get me out of the dorm. She probably hates that I'm staying inside and sleeping and writing all day while she has to go off to boring classes and talk to people. I wouldn't blame her if she did hate that.

His face seems to fall again and it almost breaks my heart.

"Fine," I say before I really think about it. "Fine, I'll go. But only for half an hour."

"Okay," he says, obviously relieved. "Thank you."

I shoot him a glare and slide out of bed. "Can you leave so I can change?"

He nods and immediately closes the door, stepping back out into the common room. I try not to slam my hand onto the nearest surface and instead open my closet, searching for the few clean pieces of clothing I still have. Eventually I find a hoodie and a pair of old sweatpants my mom bought me in middle school. They both smell like dust, but I strip off my week-old tank top and pajama pants and change.

When I come into the common room, Theo's bent over the books like he was last time he was here. A normal person would probably feel an ache of nostalgia for that time, but I don't. I feel nothing and I'm fine with it.

"I'm ready," I say. "Let's go."

He leaps up and his face breaks into a smile. Linking an arm through mine, he pulls me out the door and into the freezing November air. I shiver and wish I'd kept my dirty clothes on underneath my clean ones. The air bites my nose; Theo is annoyingly cheerful.

As we walk, he fills me in on the campus drama that I've missed. I'm only half listening, because I'm instead wondering what should happen next in my novel. I know how I want it to end but I don't know how to get there. For a moment I'm tempted to ask Theo before I remember that he was slightly shocked when I told him what it was about. I'm certain he would not approve of where the story and characters are heading.

I hear him mention Eloise's name and finally start to pay attention.

"Eloise did what?" I ask.

"She asked Jackson out, this past weekend."

"Oh. Well, good for her, I guess."

"She didn't tell you?"

"No, we haven't talked at all. Since the party."

"Oh."

He gives me a sad smile and we continue walking in silence. I keep my eyes trained on him, watching him watch his shoes. He looks extremely uncomfortable. His shoulders are rounded as if he's caving in on himself, which makes me hate him for a moment—because I'm the one who's supposed to be faltering, not him. Theo is self-assured and confident. He knows exactly who he is and doesn't care what anyone else thinks. I'm the exact opposite, and for the most part I don't really care that much about it. Spending years with only yourself as company isn't something that's hard to get used to.

"You don't have to do this, you know," I tell him.

He looks up, his eyes glassy and concerned. "Henri, I want to do this. I want to spend time with you."

"Okay."

We're quiet for a moment. He sniffs and pushes his hair back, looking past the trees to a nearby building.

"I just sometimes feel like I'm this huge black hole and everything swallows up into me," I say. "I feel like I'm just taking up space here. Because no one ever sticks around for me. I mean, my dad left us and then he died, and my mom hasn't really been around since. And friends are hard too. I've never been very good in social situations." I laugh and he gives me a pitied look. "Sorry. I don't mean to dump all of this on to you."

"It's okay," he says. "You're not dumping anything."

"Okay."

A gust of wind rushes past us and swirls the orange-red leaves around our feet. I want to stop and scoop them up to smuggle them back to my dorm but Theo keeps walking. I think he's annoyed with me.

"We're almost there," he says.

"Cove's Bakery?" I ask.

He smiles at me. "I figured it's a nice spot."

I scoff. "Right."

He grins sheepishly and digs his hands into his pockets. "It's a lot colder today than last week, isn't it?"

I shrug. "I don't know."

"Right," he says. I resist the urge to look over at him and stare. I haven't seen him in a while and he looks so out of place here—outside. His blonde hair contrasts sharply with the orange and brown around us, like summer cornered by autumn. The edges of his face seem blurry. His emotions turn into a kaleidoscope over his face. He is everything at once, and nothing at all, and then it's gone.

I begin to think I might be going crazy.

The bakery is completely empty, except for the workers behind the counter. It's a different girl than the other one the last time I was here, and she's chewing gum loudly. Her nose ring makes her look like a bull, sort of. As Theo orders for both of us, glancing up at the menu although I know it by heart, I think she really could be a bull, if she tried hard enough. Her eyes are wide and wild enough; her mouth seems almost masculine; her hair is brittle and dark. Maybe

I should write her into my novel. Maybe I should write Theo into my novel.

I look over at him, the slope of his jaw and the gentle curve of his nose. He reminds me of Eloise all of a sudden and I take a step back from him, slightly repulsed. How did I not see it before? The hair color, the feeling of summer radiating from his very skin, the assuredness and security.

He smiles at me, holding pastries in one hand and coffee in another, and motions me over to a nearby table. I can tell he wants to be a gentleman and pull out the chair for me but I sit down before he can. His similarities to Eloise are starting to settle uncomfortably in my stomach.

"You like your coffee black, right?" he asks.

I nod and grab the cup from him, taking a long sip. He grins again and drinks his own coffee, which he's probably drowned in milk and sugar. It's not even coffee anymore.

"So...how's your novel going? Have you written anything more?"

This is a pitiful attempt at conversation, but I decide to indulge him.

"It's basically all I've been doing. Writing, I mean."

"So, it's going well? You've written a lot?"

"I guess. Not really."

"Oh. Writer's block?"

"No, not really. I just take a while to write stuff. It takes time to figure things out."

"Yeah, sure."

"Yeah."

He pauses, like he doesn't know what to say, and I real-ize this is one of the few times there has been an awkward pause in one of our conversations. He's always known what to say next, and I've always continued the conversation somehow. But this is different. It's like he knows I'm starting to despise him.

"So...how's school?"

"It's fine."

"Did you get all the notes from art history?"

"Yeah. Dr. Anderson emailed them to me."

"That was nice of him."

"Yeah."

"I could've given you the notes, too, if you'd asked, you know."

"I know."

"I just—I feel bad. I know you're not feeling well, and you're missing out on a lot of class, so if there's anything—"

"It's fine. I'm all caught up. I'm thinking of going back to class next week, maybe." I'm not. It's a lie. But I want him to stop talking for a minute.

"Really?"

"Maybe."

"That's—that's good. I'm glad."

"Yeah."

He takes another sip of his barely-coffee. I watch as his forehead creases. His fingers tap the table nervously. It looks like he's about to take an exam he hasn't studied for.

"Hey, Henri? Can I ask you something?"

"Yeah."

"Are you okay? Are we okay? Because I feel like we got really close, and we talked a lot. I thought we were fine. But then you all of a sudden disappeared and kind of started to ignore me. If I did something wrong or that made you uncomfortable, I just want to know so I can fix it, because I really like talking to you. And hanging out with you."

"Nothing happened. We're fine. I just sometimes get overwhelmed with everything and need to take a break from life, I guess. This happened to me a lot in high school."

"Isn't that...not super healthy? I mean, mentally? And emotionally?"

"It's just who I am. It's not dangerous or anything, if that's what you're worried about. This is normal. For me, at least."

"Did your mom ever—"

"She didn't notice. It's fine, really."

"Okay, I'm just...okay."

I look past him, at the yellow wallpaper on the wall. The light hits it at an angle and I blink twice as it ripples slightly. I look at Theo, then smile, but it doesn't reach my eyes. He doesn't notice. Of course he doesn't.

I turn my attention back to the wallpaper, at the pattern as it curves up and down and writhes and twists like it's trying to escape. It's a sickly color, but the faces inside make up for it. I've never really liked abstract art but after seeing the wallpaper this time I wonder if maybe my opinions have changed, because I can't take my eyes off of it as I try to decipher what it's trying to tell me. The faces morph into bodies and shapes and animals, all convulsing sporadically into one large masterpiece. It's beautiful despite its irregularity and chaos.

A figure bounds to the left, towards the window. Another leaps across the top of the wooden shelves into the kitchen and it doesn't come back out. The last figure, bobbing up and down on the wall with three heads and countless limbs, stares directly at me. The eyes change back and forth between circles and half-moons, looking to the door and to me. I understand: it wants me to leave.

Instead of saying anything, which I would rather do but know Theo would find even more worrying, I duck my chin slightly to acknowledge that I've heard the wallpaper.

Theo isn't paying attention to me. He's staring out the window, fully immersed in watching a tiny dog outside of the window as it sniffs a tree and lifts its nose into the breeze.

"I think I have to go," I say.

He snaps back. "What? But we just got here."

"I have some notes I have to finish, and a paper. I forgot."

"I—oh. Okay."

"Yeah. Thanks for this, though. I'll call you sometime, okay?"

"Sure. Please do, Henri."

"You don't need to worry about me. I'm fine. Really."

"I know. I'll see you later. Or talk to you later."

"Yeah, bye."

I stand and see the wallpaper return to normal. As I head to the door, a sense of pride fills my chest. It chose me. The wallpaper chose me to speak to and I listened, just as I should.

Adelaide's mother is not home when she arrives at the run-down house. She pauses before unlocking the front door, glancing at the wet stack of wood next to the front door and the red rocking chair at the end of the porch. A wave of anger rises in her chest: this is her house, her childhood. What right did her mother have to destroy a home like this, while under the gaze of her and her father's eyes?

She slides the key into the lock and turns it. The door opens with a sickening creak. Adelaide stands in the doorway and realizes the smell of bleach is still lingering in the air. Her nose wrinkles as she takes a slow step inside, mind racing but quiet at the same time.

Her father is everywhere. Her mother's infidelity is everywhere.

Her eyes land on the painting she was obsessed with as a kid, the one of an old town house in the middle of rural nowhere. She wants to run a hand over the uneven wooden frame but knows she shouldn't, because the last time she did a splinter wound up burrowing itself in the palm of her hand. There are flashes of her mother and her father and her in the living room—watching TV, playing board games, her first underage drink with them sitting by her side and laughing as she spat it out in disgust.

She wonders how far back it went. She wonders how long her mother was keeping it from them, how long she was sneaking that man in and out of their house. And most of all, she wonders how her father did not know. Because he was the kind of person who read dozens of mysteries and true crime books. He knew how the human mind worked and still he could not decipher his own wife. He was the smartest man Adelaide knew. And the stupidest.

As she thinks more about this, the front door wide open behind her, the memories begin to fade and in their places settle visions of the man and her mother. This foyer; the couch; the stools in the kitchen; the sink; the little room where the washing machine lived. Had her mother made him meals, or had she ushered him out as soon as possible? Had they watched movies together, or had her mother not wanted to know the man?

Adelaide knew the man. Of course she did—he had worked with her father. It makes her even more angry that she knew and trusted him, but she reminds herself that it's her mother's fault; it has to be. Because if it's not, then what she's about to do would be entirely unjust and wrong.

The visions don't fade—instead, they seem to become more vivid and real. Bile rises in her throat. And so she makes a decision, the only one she knows how to make.

She starts with the painting. Her fingers grip the top of the frame and in a single motion she pulls it to the ground, shattering the glass on the floor. It doesn't matter that the actual painting isn't damaged; the glass is enough.

Next is the living room. She drags the TV to the ground, overturns the couch, smashes the coffee table to pieces, wipes her muddy wet shoes on the carpet. The room is no longer full of her own memories, or the made-up ones, even if she can't differentiate the two. Now it is just a delightful mess of her own creation and she gladdens at the thought of her mother walking in and seeing what she's done.

The boost of adrenaline carries her over to the kitchen, where she opens all of the cupboards and breaks the plates and bowls and cups over the counter, letting them shatter onto the ground. She tears up the paper napkins one by one and scatters them on the island.

When she's finally satisfied with it, she enters the room with the washing machine. For a minute she doesn't know how to ruin this one, but then she gets an idea. Without breaking a sweat she overturns the two machines, going back to the kitchen for a carton of eggs in the fridge. She brings them back to the room and hurls them onto the milky white surface, watching in glee as the yolks stream down the side of the machine.

She steps out of the room and examines the catastrophe of her revenge. It looks pathetic compared to what she feels inside, and she *decides then and there that it's not enough. No matter how much she tries to damage this house, it will never be enough.*

The front steps creak and someone stands in the doorway. Adelaide turns on her heels. Her mother is there, the gloomy weather behind her highlighting her haggard outline. Adelaide watches her eyes glaze over and reach her.

"How could you do this?" Adelaide's mother asks.

She knows exactly what she has to do.

"Henri. Henri."

I open my eyes and sit up in bed. For a moment I'm disoriented—my shutters are closed and it's pitch black, except for the glow of my alarm clock beside me. I don't know how many days or nights have passed. I lost count after Theo took me to the café and now I don't care.

The clock reads 3:54 PM. My head turns to the door as another knock sounds.

"What, Clary?"

She gives a long sigh. "Are you going to clean up the mess in the kitchen?"

I repress a groan but lie back down and flip over. "Yeah."

"Henri, this place is a mess. You don't clean up after yourself, and I have too much work to do it for you, okay? Can you just please make sure you don't leave a mess anywhere?"

"Yeah."

"Henri, I'm serious. If you don't start, I'm going to ask you to leave for a while. I need a break from all this."

That catches my attention. I roll onto my back and stare at the sliver of light from underneath the door. Clary's feet make little shadows.

"You can't kick me out."

"Yeah, I can," she says. "I can't live in a pigsty anymore."

"It's not that messy, Clary. You're overreacting."

"I think *you're* overreacting. Look, I don't know what happened with your mom or whatever, but it's not okay to leave the kitchen like that. I live here too."

"I'm not overreacting," I grumble before pulling the covers back over my head.

"I am going to kick you out if things don't change." She shifts her weight from one foot to the other. "I love you and I really want you to get better, but this isn't working for me right now."

"Okay, jeez."

"What?" she says. "I can't hear you."

I sigh and take the blankets off my head. "I said '*okay, jeez.*'"

"Okay."

Her footsteps tread away. I stare up at the ceiling, angry now. She has no right to kick me out of here. It's my dorm room too, even if her father did build this entire building. If I could move my limbs I would get out of this bed and go scream at Clary. Instead I settle for doing it in my head.

It's quiet for a moment. Then I hear a gasp—Clary being dramatic again—and heavy footsteps toward my door. I rub my hand along my forehead. I really don't want to deal with Clary again.

She knocks loudly.

"Yes, Clary?" I say, just to annoy her.

This time she actually comes in. The door opens in a rush

and all the light streams in. I groan and roll over, clenching my eyes shut.

"Close the door!" I say.

"*No*," she snaps. "No, this is insane! You've been in bed, in the same position, for days, Henri! You leave the kitchen a mess and now you're putting my clean clothes on the ground? Why on earth would you do that, Henri? You're literally not even washing any clothes! Why did you take my *clean* clothes from the washing machine and *throw* them on the floor?"

"I didn't!" I say from beneath the covers. I curl up into a ball. I don't want to deal with this right now; it's giving me a headache.

"Henri. Why did you—"

"I *didn't*, I swear!"

"Oh, so we have a ghost, then, Henri? Really? Come on, please! You're one of my best friends, Henri. Why are you treating me like this now?"

"I'm not trying to hurt you," I say.

"You're hurting me by hurting yourself. You need to take care of yourself and you're just neglecting everything. When was the last time you went to class, Henri?"

"I get notes from my professors. They understand."

She shakes her head—I can hear it. "You need to go to class. The notes aren't enough."

"I'm doing *fine*. I can always catch up."

"Henri, what is wrong? Can you please just talk to me?"

"You were mad at me two seconds ago," I say. "How come you're being so nice now?"

She gives a long sigh. "I'm being nice now because I know this isn't you."

"Maybe it is, Clary. Maybe this is me and you and everyone else have just been ignoring it this entire time."

"Henri."

"I'm serious!"

"Stop it."

"You have no right to tell me who I am and who I'm not, okay? I know exactly who I am. And this is it. So if you don't like it or can't live with it, then, fine, kick me out."

"I will," she says angrily. "I will. I'm serious."

"So am I."

"Okay, fine! Leave. Right now. Get your stuff and go, and come back only when you've decided to start taking care of yourself and your stuff again, because I really can't do this anymore."

She peels the covers off me, leaning over and staring at me with a look in her eyes I've never seen before. This isn't the Clary I know.

"Get out of my dorm, Henri."

She's serious.

"If you were really my friend you wouldn't kick me out," I say.

"I love you, but not that much. I'm sick and tired of putting your needs before my own. I stomached this for a month. I let you leave the kitchen a mess and I cleaned up after you. I didn't care if you didn't go to class at all. I let you stink up this entire dorm because you don't shower anymore. But I'm so tired of it. I'm so, so tired. I need a break."

I realize how cold it's gotten since I last went outside when I leave the dorm building with only a backpack. My first steps are cautious, like I'm about to fall down the stairs. I don't fall.

But I do amble slowly, trying to lengthen the amount of time I have until I get to my mother's house in town. I'm hoping she's not home but I know she will be; where else would she be at this time of day? She doesn't have a job anymore and Dahlia makes it clear she doesn't need her help for anything.

When I think of my sister I can almost feel myself bristle, which only makes me more angry, because she's my sister and I shouldn't be uncomfortable around her.

I think about Adelaide as I meander around campus. What would she do in this kind of situation? Would she confront her sister, as Theo told me to? Or would she take my approach, more of a wait-out-the-situation kind of thing in hopes that it'll be resolved on its own?

My pondering doesn't really matter, because I already know what she would do.

I stop walking without knowing why. The sky looks small from down here, birds like ants scattered across the blue. I wish I could be poetic and say I wanted to be one of them— the birds, I mean. Not an ant. I don't think I'd ever want to be an ant.

Lots of writers have talked (or written) about being different animals. Birds are a common theme, and I can see why: the perceived freedom, the ability to look down on the world with a pretentiousness most writers are born with. But if I were a bird, all I would think about would be crashing back down into the forgotten earth in a fiery finale. And thinking about my impending death isn't something I find enjoyable.

If I were a bird.

Another lonely figure appears from the autumn gloom. I spot it too late—by the time I realize there's another person on the path, they've already seen me and I can't go running into the mist now, because it would be obvious I was avoiding them. So I continue walking, keeping my head down and eyes trained on my shoes as the person nears me.

"Henri?" I hear.

I look up. "Oh—Dr. O'Kelly."

"It's good to see you," he says. He's tilted to one side, a huge stack of books tucked under one arm. His trenchcoat gathers at his ankles; he looks like a character from a mystery novel, especially in this weather. "How's your novel going?"

"My—sorry?"

"Your novel. You emailed me a few weeks ago, explaining that you've been inside writing all day. That's why you're not attending classes?" He smiles. "The Great American Novel demands to be written, eh?"

God I hate him. "Oh—yes." I feign a laugh. "Yes, I've been busy. Writing. A lot."

"Good, good. How far into it are you?"

"Well, it's hard to say. I don't—I don't plot. You know that."

"Right," he nods.

"So I don't know how long it'll be."

"Did you clear up on those themes we talked about?" He gives me what looks like a half-wink and I desperately want to slap him across the face.

"Um...no, I'm still working on it. I'm just waiting to see where my writing leads me."

"Hm." He frowns slightly. "Well, if you ever want to stop

by or come to class to discuss your work, know you're always welcome to."

"Yeah. Thanks."

"Right. Well, I'll see you later, possibly. Have a good rest of your day."

"You as well," I say, eager to get out of this conversation.

He nods and sets off again, humming quietly. I watch him go: this little penguin waddle he does. I wonder how he got hired here. I wonder how any writing teacher got hired, because in my mind writing isn't something that can be taught. It's like a disease. It spreads until it takes you over and by then it's too late, and you can't teach passion like that.

I think about this as I walk through campus, in a direct line this time. I don't avoid the campus gates anymore. I don't know what will face me at home—fighting or crying or screaming or silence—but at this point I'm too exhausted to be worried. Despite sleeping for a dozen hours each day, my eyelids feel heavy, like water.

My mind returns to Theo, like it always does. He's probably mad. Or upset. Likely offended and confused. I don't think the image of his face as I left the coffee shop will ever escape my mind, because all I see when I think of him is the worried lines on his forehead, the scrunched-up eyebrows in a manner that makes him seem boyish, the wringing hands underneath the table, the wallpaper behind him, smirking as he shivers. It fills me with pride, that image. Maybe I'm a sociopath, but I liked knowing I could do that to somebody; I liked knowing I could hurt someone just as much as they hurt me.

The house, though quiet, isn't empty when I arrive. I put

my bag down by the front door and take off my coat. Through the window is my mother in the backyard, staring at the rose bushes against the fence.

I frown, adjust my hair because I know she'll comment on how messy it is if I don't, and walk through the kitchen until I reach the door.

She turns suddenly, spotting me through the glass. Her face becomes animated and she ushers me outside with a gloved hand. At least she still has enough sense to put gloves on.

I sigh but open the door and join her, immediately regretting leaving my coat inside. But there's nothing I can do about it now, because she has grabbed my hand and is pulling me over to the bushes, pointing at a bud.

"Look!" she says. "It's dead!"

I pull my hand away and straighten. "Yeah. You probably let it flood, with all this rain."

She scoffs and waves a hand in the air. Her makeup is messy. Smudged eyeliner that she clearly slept in, blush that hasn't been rubbed in all the way, chalky concealer underneath her eyes, bright red lipstick that curls inward along with her lips.

"I didn't drown it," she insists. "I didn't drown it, of course I didn't. I love these plants. I love all of them. Especially the roses." She says this last part in a baby voice, like how you'd speak to a dog. "Of course I kept them alive. I take good care of all my plants."

"I know, Mom," I say. "Look, I need to talk to you about something important, okay? Could we go inside? It's freezing out here."

"Of course, Henri. Why didn't you bring a coat out with you?"

I suppress a crude response and walk behind her as she leads me back to the house, the skirt of her dress dragging uncomfortably on the wet grass.

She looks back at me and eyes my outfit. "Your hair is a mess, Henri. You should really brush it more."

I ignore this bit but she knows I heard it.

When we're finally inside, my mother takes ages to take off her gloves, then her coat, then her hat, then her hairnet, then her shoes, then her socks, then another vest she'd put on over a summer dress. She places each item neatly on her bed, and once they're all together she takes them one by one to her dresser or her closet. From there, she makes sure they're put in the exact position she found them in.

She seems to sense my impatience. She turns and smiles.

"Would you like some tea?"

"No, Mom, I really need to talk to you."

She sits down on the bed heavily. "About what?"

"My roommate kicked me out."

"What?" she says absentmindedly.

"I don't know. She just didn't want me there anymore, I guess. So she told me to leave, and I did. But I need to stay here until I can find another place to live. Is that okay?"

"Of course, of course. Anything you need, Henri. You've always known that."

"Yeah, sure." I hesitate. "Thank you. This is really helpful."

She gives me a bashful look. "I just hope you won't mind living with Dahlia again."

My teeth grind against each other when I hear her name.

"Yeah," I say in a tight voice, "it's fine. We'll be fine. You don't need to worry about that."

"Right," she chuckles.

"When's she coming home, anyway?"

"Oh, I don't know. In an hour, I suppose? Her school ended half an hour ago but she normally goes over to friends' houses to study."

I highly doubt that's what she's doing but I don't say anything. "Okay. Do you need me to do anything? Get groceries, coffee?"

"You're my daughter, not my servant."

"I know," I say, "but I feel like I should be doing something to earn my stay here."

"You're my daughter, Henri."

"I know, but I—"

"You don't need to do anything extra. I'm happy to have you here."

She looks up at me, face suddenly bright. It reminds me of before.

Dahlia comes home late that night. By that time I've already started to hear my mother's voice inside my head as well as her actual voice outside, and the shadows around the house assume menacing forms. But I don't tell my family that. They wouldn't understand.

She comes home in a flurry, complaining about how much homework she has and how annoying her friends are. When she sees me she pauses for a moment but then returns to her yammering. She doesn't even ask how I am, or how our mother's day was.

Dinner is fraught with tension. I order in Chinese food, an old favorite, but it doesn't feel the same. Normally we would crowd around the TV and watch some game show. This time, my mother demands we eat around the dining table like a real family. She says we haven't had a real family dinner in over a year so now is the perfect time. I think Dahlia and I both disagree with this sentiment.

And she brings out her wedding china for us to eat on, lights two taper candles and gets champagne from the fridge. I don't look at the expiration date on the bottle.

"Why do you still have all this stuff?" Dahlia asks, looking pointedly at the china.

"It's not like I can just give all this away," our mother says. "It's wedding china. It was a gift."

"Yeah, for you and Dad. But after—"

"Dahlia," I warn.

"Fine, jeez."

She grabs a few boxes of food and pours their contents onto her plate: plain white rice, steamed broccoli, dumplings. She then continues to drown her entire plate in soy sauce, just like she used to. A flicker of nostalgia bursts up but I quickly push it down. I don't want to think of Dahlia as my little sister when she's so awful to our mother.

We eat in an uncomfortable silence. Our mother stares off into space, probably thinking of the last time we did this—and how much happier it was—or the photo albums she still has to look through.

"Mom," I say, just to cut through the quiet. She looks at me, eyes blank for a moment. "How was your day today?"

She smiles. "It was wonderful. I have my two daughters together at the same table again."

Dahlia and I glance at each other and look away. My eyes land on a dark wood cabinet a few feet away, and the shadows beside it. They twist suddenly, writhing in place like the wallpaper at the coffee shop with Theo. I stare at them with a fascinated horror.

This used to happen to me all the time, back when I was still in high school. I told a friend about it and she never talked to me again, so I quickly learned not to say anything when I saw something like this. No one else would understand it. I got the sense it was a gift—but a dangerous one. If anyone knew what I could do, I was sure they would try to take it away. Or study it in a lab and pick apart my brain.

The shadow this time isn't menacing, but it's unnerving to have it so close to my mother. It emerges from the darkness and I recognize the outline immediately.

I stand. "I think I'm going to go to bed. I have some homework I need to do."

My mother nods and Dahlia doesn't look up from her food. I leave my plate, hoping my father will follow me instead of staying with them. And he does.

He doesn't make a sound as he follows me down the narrow hallway to my old bedroom. I open the door, waiting for him to come inside, but he stays still. He doesn't want to come in.

"What do you want?" I whisper. I have no idea if I say it out loud or only in my head. "What do you want? Can you please leave me alone?"

He's silent.

"Please?"

I close my eyes for a second, then open them, and he's gone. I let out a sigh, not sure if it's relief or disappointment, because I *like* feeling special. I like feeling like otherworldly, cerebral things—creatures or beings or whatever they are—have chosen me as the person they show themselves to. I feel like a messenger. Or a prophet. Then I begin to think maybe I should be worshipping these creatures; maybe they are really divine spirits. Or maybe I can just see the dead.

Dahlia's voice cuts into my head. "You're always so terrible to me."

"What?" my mother says meekly. I can almost hear her take a sip of wine; she's trying to escape this conversation.

"I know you try to hide it, but it's really so obvious that you love Henri more than you love me."

"Oh, Dahlia, that's not tr—"

"Stop it, Mom," she snaps. "I mean it. This is so humiliating for me, do you even understand that? My friends come over here and all you talk about is your perfect daughter who's going to grow up to be a world-famous author some day. You never once mention me. You never once stop to think about how I feel about all of this. And you're really letting her stay here while she fails out of school? How exactly is that teaching her a good lesson?"

I hear my mother shift in her seat.

"Seriously, Mom, it's really terrible. You're the reason I'm not doing well in school right now, do you know that? I have to clean up after all of your messes and take care of you and this house when I'm only a teenager. I'm supposed to be the kid, Mom. You're supposed to be taking care of me, not the other way around. I can't focus on my classes because of you. It's so unfair that Henri just gets to go to school and not worry about you at all, while I'm here all the time with you."

"She—"

"I really don't want to hear it right now. You always defend her, even when I'm trying to tell you how she's hurt me."

"Henri didn't mean for—"

"Oh, sure, I know she didn't. She's perfect, right?"

"No, she's not, Dahlia," my mom says. "She's not, but she does take care of me. She brings me pastries and coffee and she visits me as much as she can, with her schoolwork and all, and—"

Dahlia slams her fist onto the table, and I jump back in surprise. The noise rattles through the house.

"*I hate you*," she says loudly. "You can't even begin to understand what is *wrong* with you. It's not my fault Dad left, okay? It's so unfair for you to tear your life to pieces and drag me down with you. Why can't you go to therapy or something? Or is all that money paying for Henri's tuition?"

"Dahlia—"

"*Stop* it! I'm serious!"

"Dahlia"—my mother has started to cry, I can hear it in her voice—"I *don't* love Henri more than you, you know that, don't you?"

"No!" Dahlia shouts. I flinch away from the door. "No, I don't know that! Because whatever you do, it's always about her and it's never about me! You never care about me, and I don't think you ever did."

"That's just not—"

"*Stop* it!"

"That's just not true, Dahlia. I love you both equally, in different ways. Please don't get upset. Please don't cry. We were having such a lovely night." A chair squeaks—probably my mother going over to sit next to Dahlia. I want to tell her it's a lost cause. "We were having such a lovely night," she repeats. "It's almost like your father was here with us. Do you remember our old family dinners? It was just like that. I wish you and Henri would get over this disagreement you seem to have. I really wish you would. You're sisters, Dahlia, and all you have is each other. Dahlia? Are you listening to me?"

She doesn't respond.

"Dahlia, please. Please don't be mad. I just want to talk to you."

Again, she stays quiet.

"Lia, come on. Are you listening to me?"

"Just leave me alone," Dahlia says in a low voice.

"Please—"

"Just leave me alone!" Her voice raises to a yell. "I *said*, just leave me *alone!*"

That's when I open the door and rush into the hallway, coming out on the other side to see my mother, forlorn in her seat, next to Dahlia, who is fuming and looks like she could explode. Neither of them notice me in the dark.

"Dahlia, you can't just—"

"Yes, I can! You have absolutely no right to tell me what to do. You're literally just a depressed alcoholic. You're a pitiful excuse for a mother."

My mother recoils in her seat. It looks like she's been afraid to hear those words, and now that she has she doesn't know how to react. Dahlia's face exudes pride and I hate her in that moment.

"I can't believe you'd treat your own daughter like this," Dahlia says. "I can't believe you'd completely ignore my own needs and—"

"Don't talk to me like that, Dahlia," my mom whispers.

"*What?*"

"I know I'm not perfect. I know. But it's not fair to speak to—"

"It's not *fair*? It's not *fair*, really? I think it's pretty fair for me to tell you what you're doing wrong. You seriously can't expect me to just sit back and watch you treat Henri like some kind of a god and me like—"

"I don't treat Henri like—"

"Yes you *do*, Mom, you—"

"I *don't* treat—"

"Yes, you—"

"Dahlia, I do not—"

"*Don't* talk to me like that!" Dahlia shouts. "You have *no right* to talk to me like that! You're so—God, you're so—so—*I hate you*! I hate you, I *hate* you!"

"Do not—"

I hear a sickening slap and then a thump; my mother falling back into her chair, stunned.

The world slows and I forget how to move for a second, but at some point I'm on the street, shivering in the snow without my coat, stumbling back to campus. I don't even think about what Clary will say when she sees me again. All I can think about is getting out of that house with its suffocating walls and away from Dahlia, because I don't know if I can even call her my sister again.

I know it's too late. I know it's far too late to help my mother.

"How could you do this?" her mother repeats.

Adelaide shakes her head. "You know exactly how. You and—and Bill—know exactly how."

It dawns on her mother. Adelaide watches in a kind of half-terrified, half-joyful glee as the realization spreads over her face.

"Oh—oh, Adelaide," she begins. "I—"

"How? Is that what you're about to ask? How on earth did your idiot of a child find out about your affair?"

"I—"

"Yeah, I'm sure that's what you're about to ask. You want to hear how? The eighty-year-old neighbor wrote me a letter, that's how. He wrote me a letter and explained to me exactly what happened and how much of it he saw."

"That's no reason to destroy this—"

"Yes, it is!" Adelaide says, her voice rising. "Of course it is a reason! It's an entirely justifiable reason!"

"Adelaide—"

"No. No, don't you dare say my name. Don't you dare."

"Adelaide," her mother says sharply. "Bill and I—we fooled around a bit, yes. And I admit it was immature. I admit it was a mistake, and I have the rest of my life to feel sorry about it. But—"

"No," Adelaide says. "Are you serious? That's not an excuse. You 'fooled around'? You're not a teenager anymore. You don't get to just 'fool around' whenever you feel like it. You have a daughter. You

had a husband. Did you even stop to think for a second what it would do to our lives?"

"Of course I thought about it."

"Then why the hell didn't you stop?"

"Because—Adelaide, look. I don't expect you to understand this at your age. But—but marriage is hard. It's really, really hard. Movies and books make a big show of romance and passion, but after a certain point that fades and all you're left with is hard work. And I—I wasn't willing to put in the work. Your father was. Of course he was. But I missed the romance and the butterflies in my stomach and I found that when I was with Bill. I didn't know what to do. I just knew with him it felt right so I didn't stop it. But you have to understand I wish I could go back and change what I did."

"You're only saying that because Dad's dead now."

"No, I'm not."

"I don't care. I don't care anymore. You still cheated. You're still a terrible wife."

"I was not a terrible wife."

"So sleeping with another man equates to being—"

"Adelaide Montgomery, do not say—"

"Don't tell me what I can and can't say! I'm an adult now and you're a cheater. I should just staple the letter 'A' across your forehead."

"You think you're so smart, do you?" Her mother's eyes narrow to slits. "You think that because you go to college, because you're so educated, you can say whatever you want to me and expect me to take it?"

"I never said—"

"You're not that smart, Adelaide," her mother snarls. "You're not. Did you know we almost held you back a grade in elementary school because you failed every single math test you ever took? Did you know that, Adelaide? Did you know a teacher wanted to have you tested for a learning disability? Did you know multiple teachers have asked me if I thought it was really a good idea to place you in rigorous classes?"

"That's not true."

"Yes, Adelaide, it is. You're not the genius you want everyone to think you are. Your books are meaningless. Your words are meaningless. When it comes down to it, when it really comes down to it, your education has no value in your life. You are nothing without your ego, Adelaide. I've always known that."

"You're terrible," Adelaide says. "How could you say that to your daughter?"

"How could you destroy your mother's house by the words of an old man?"

"You admitted to it."

"Maybe, but you're not smart enough to understand why I did what I did."

"Don't—"

"Your father fought with me, of course he did. He insisted you were smart. He thought I was pushing you too hard when I was really trying to lighten your workload because you obviously couldn't handle the classes you were taking. Your father isn't here anymore, Adelaide. He's not here to defend you anymore. And I am sick and tired of hearing you lord your education over me, education that I paid for, education that will teach you next to nothing about surviving, while you expect me to sit back and worship you at your feet. I never would have had a child if I'd known what she would be like. I never would have."

Adelaide is crying now. She came here thinking she would have the upper hand—knowing *she would have the upper hand*—but now she doesn't know what to say. Her tears fall in fat streams down her cheeks and she knows what her mother is going to say next, because she said it every single time Adelaide started to cry.

"You are too sensitive, Adelaide. You can't cry whenever you feel like it. It won't get you what you want, not in this house. It certainly won't."

"I'm not—"

"I wish you could see this all from my perspective. I wish you could have seen the years I spent agonizing over my own daughter's stupidity, knowing there was nothing I could do to change it. You're going to fail, Adelaide. You were always going to fail."

The tears slowly dry up, crackling hot anger replacing them. Adelaide's skin is burning. She looks at her mother and imagines ripping the flesh from the bone in strips, just to hear her mother scream and cry at her feet. She will make her mother worship her. She will make her beg for death, like all of the villains in the books she's read. She's done being the hero. She's done being the perfect daughter—or the illusion of it—and now just wants to make her mother hurt.

Adelaide leaps at her. Hands tighten in midair and she lands with a crash, her mother flung to the ground. She shouts in pain (something about her back) before Adelaide scrambles on top of her like a wild animal and pulls at her hair.

She can feel the brittle strands being torn from her scalp and almost laughs at the sound. Some of it coils around her fingers like snakes but she ignores it, instead grabbing her mother's skull and bashing it into the ground, back up to her face so they stare into each other's eyes—Adelaide savoring the look of terror—and then slamming her head back down as hard as she possibly can.

They are no longer mother and daughter. They are ape and ape, white hot rage and growls that fill the house.

Adelaide counts each indent her mother's head makes into the floor: one, two, three, four, five...

She doesn't want it to end. And at this point it looks like it might not end, because her mother is holding on to whatever shred of life she still has, her arms flailing in the air and her hands coming up empty.

"Shut up!" Adelaide shouts. "Shut up, shut up, shut up!"

Her mother does not. Instead, she screams louder and smacks her daughter alongside her head, stunning her for a moment before she returns to the primal bashing.

Adelaide yells between her mother's exclamations. "You—did—this—to—me!"

She decides she's not hitting her mother's head hard enough because she's still making noise, so she drags her up by the hair (rather, the little that is left) and brings her to the kitchen, where she forces her to her knees.

"You said I want you to worship at my feet," Adelaide spits. "So do it. Worship at my feet."

Adelaide lets go and her mother slumps to the floor, head slamming onto Adelaide's shoes dumbly.

She bends down and pulls her head to the side, whispering into her ear. "You're wrong. You're wrong about me. I'm smart. Because I'm going to kill you and no one is ever going to find out."

Her mother, barely conscious, moves her head slightly. Her voice is raspy and quiet. Adelaide has to strain to hear the words.

"I've killed a man," she heaves. "I've killed a man, and no one will ever find him."

She dies with a smile on her lips.

A knock sounds on my door. I haven't slept in what feels like days and my eyes are dry when I open them slightly wider.

"Yeah?" I say.

"It's me. It's Clary."

"Yeah?"

"I—I made pancakes," she says lamely. "Chocolate chip. With coffee. And the 80s rock station is on the radio. To welcome you back, I guess. If you...want to come out."

"I'm fine in here."

I hear her slump against the door and imagine her forehead against the wood. A small part of me feels bad, but then I remember what the world outside of my dark room is. I remember that my father wants me to stay in here.

"Henri, please. It's not healthy to stay inside all day. Can you just open your window? The shutters? It's snowing. It's the first snow of the season."

"I don't care."

"You used to."

"I don't anymore, okay? Can you just leave me alone now? I'm trying to sleep."

Dejected, she moves away from the door. "Okay."

When I hear her footsteps retreat I sigh and roll over in my bed. She doesn't understand it—no one does. If I go outside I have to face outside and right now that seems like the hardest thing in the world. I'd rather stay in my bed, under the covers, where my dad can't bother me, where Dahlia can't scream in my ears. It's safe here.

But Clary is right; I do love the first snow of the season.

And my back hurts, so I should probably stretch it or something.

I pull the covers off my body and lay shivering in bed for a few moments before finally mustering the strength to heave myself out and pad over to the window. I reach up and open the shutters.

White. That's all I see. The ground is white, the buildings are white, the trees are white, even the sky is white. It makes me want to sit at my desk and write but I can't. Because if I start to write, I'll think about all the great writers and novels already out there, and I'll think about what they thought winter and snow symbolizes—rebirth, purity, *hope*—and I don't know how to tell an entire history of writers that they're completely wrong. That winter doesn't symbolize reincarnation; it symbolizes death.

I pull the shutters closed again.

Hours go by. At least I think it's hours. Maybe it's just one. Maybe it's a day. I took my alarm clock from my room and emptied the batteries into the trash a few weeks ago because the noise was annoying me and I hated pressing the snooze button over and over again each morning. It made me feel lazy.

I try to resist the temptation of getting out my phone and spending hours surfing the internet even though I know it would distract me from the constant war inside my head, all of the thoughts I can't ignore anymore.

But I can't ignore the ringing from the top drawer of my desk.

I groan and grab the phone in one movement, slumping

back into bed once I have it in my hand. I pause when I see the caller ID.

"What?" I say.

"What took you so long? I've been calling for the last hour." She sounds different.

"Dahlia, I'm trying to sleep. Can you please hurry up?"

"It's Mom."

I sit up in bed, heart suddenly racing. "What about Mom? Did something happen?"

"I—" Her voice hiccups. "She..."

"Dahlia, tell me. What happened?"

"She...she's dead, Henri. She died."

"*What*?"

"I don't know, it just happened." She's full-on sobbing now. Trying to be the victim like always. "She was in the living room and I just walked out there and she—she wasn't moving so I called the cops but they took forever to come and I didn't know what to do so I stayed away from her because she looked so wrong and so pale and I didn't—"

"Stop it," I say. "Stop talking. Be quiet."

"Henri?"

"Shut up."

I was expecting a different reaction to the news of my mother's death. I thought I would be wild, or silent. I thought my heart would be torn from my chest and I'd never be able to put it back in again, that I'd be broken or hollow forever. I imagined an eternal ache in my body that I would eventually succumb to, and I'd think it was the most romantic thing to ever occur. I thought I would turn my mother's death into poetry. I thought I would stir up passion with my words and ease my own pain.

But now I'm just empty. I feel nothing, I breathe nothing.

Until a single emotion rushes up from my stomach into my throat and bile fills my mouth.

"You did this," I spit.

Dahlia's breath shakes over the phone. "What?"

"You did this. You killed her. You killed my mother."

"What? Henri?"

"Don't try to deny it. You know you did. You drove her to this point, where she thought there was no other way out."

"No, Henri, she—"

"Don't you dare cry. Don't you dare play the victim. You're a murderer. You killed my mother."

"Henri—"

"Do you seriously think what you said to her had no impact? She worshipped you, Dahlia. She was on her hands and knees and was ready to kiss the very floor you stepped on. She gave everything to you and you abused her in return. What kind of daughter abuses her own mother?"

"I didn't—"

"Don't deny it. You made her feel worthless, you made her feel pain emotional and physical."

"No, I—"

"I hate you. I fucking hate you. You killed my mother and you're not my sister. You never have been."

"Henri—"

I hang up.

The poets are wrong. Death doesn't turn you into a gentler,

more forgiving person. It turns you bitter. It turns you into the kind of person your mother would despise, but it doesn't matter now because your mother is gone and she's not here to tell you how you should be.

It turns you into the kind of person who wants to kill your little sister.

But you can't do that. You're not a character in one of your novels. Instead, you're sitting in your dorm room, trying to suffocate yourself underneath the covers as a boy you once thought you loved knocks on the door and begs you to open it, because—get this—he has a surprise.

And so you yell at him to come inside, and he does, and you're reminded that you do love him, probably. And then you feel bad for yelling at him. But you shouldn't feel bad, not really, because your mother was just murdered by her daughter(s) and shouldn't that give you some kind of leeway when it comes to your anger?

It doesn't seem to phase him. The yelling, I mean.

"I brought you a book, Henri," he says happily. "It's *The Picture of Dorian Gray*. The leather-bound one. You said you liked leather-bound books in the bookstore, remember?"

"I already have a copy of it."

"But you said that you'll buy—"

"Well, I changed my mind. Okay? I realized how pretentious and stupid and wasteful that was, so I threw out all of my extra copies of my books. I don't need another *Dorian Gray*. I already have one."

"What?"

"What, 'what'?"

"What do you mean you threw out all your extra copies? You threw out your books?"

"Only the second or third copies, Theo. It's not a big deal."

"Not a big deal? Henri, you threw out books?"

"Yes. What is your problem?"

"*You* threw out books?"

"I don't see what the problem is. It isn't like I threw them in the trash. I had Clary drop them off at a Goodwill for me."

"And she didn't think that was strange?" His eyebrows are clenched together.

"Of course not. Why would she?"

"Henri, you never donate books. You never get rid of them. You told me...you told me you wanted to keep every single book you've ever read and that's why you don't like libraries that much."

"I like the idea of libraries," I grumble. What kind of person is he to bring this up right now?

"I know you do. I know. I just—"

"My mom died," I say.

He's quiet. "What?"

"Jesus Christ, are you deaf? I said my mom died."

Shock spreads over his face, then sadness. "Henri...why didn't you tell me?"

I almost scoff at him. "Because you wouldn't understand."

"Maybe—maybe not, but I could have been here. I could have...how long?"

"I don't know. Two days ago, maybe. Maybe less."

"Why didn't you tell me?"

"Why are you making me feel guilty for not telling you?

Was I supposed to call you immediately after I found out, or something?"

"N-No. I just feel bad. That you've been here by yourself."

"I like being by myself."

"I know, just—"

"You know the novel I was writing?" I interrupt, abruptly sitting up in bed and pulling the covers off me. I slide socks onto my clammy feet.

I can tell he thinks this is an odd thing to bring up at a moment like this, but at this point I don't care anymore.

"Yes."

"Well, it's not a novel. I found out it was more like a short story. But I finished it, anyway. Do you want to see it?"

His head moves up and down like he's not sure if he actually wants to. And I don't blame him. I haven't slept in two days and I haven't showered in even longer. I'm honestly surprised he has tolerated me for this long already.

Silently I cross the room and take a few pieces of paper from the top of my desk. Theo holds out his hands, expecting me to hand the manuscript over to him, but I just stare at it.

"This is it," I say. "It's not very long."

"Yeah," he agrees.

"You want to know the worst part about it?"

"What?"

"It took me a few months to write. But in the end, I hated it anyway. I hate it."

"Wait, Henri—"

"Do you have a lighter on you?"

He looks at me, his eyes reflecting mine. "I..."

"I know you do."

Sheepishly, he digs into the pocket of his trousers and produces a bright pink lighter he probably bought from a drug store. I ignore a slight pang of sorrow when I realize it's the same one my dad used to use whenever he lit a cigarette on the weekends. He only ever smoked when the entire family was around.

I take the lighter from Theo's sweaty fingers and struggle to work it, pushing Theo away when he offers to help.

I gaze at the words on the cover page one last time: "Adelaide Montgomery's father is dead." And I realize, for the first time, that maybe Adelaide is not so fictional after all.

The flame is tender at first, almost caressing the paper, before it engulfs it entirely. It's like we're both hypnotized by the fire inside of this tiny and otherwise dark room but when Theo notices that I have no intention of taking my hand away or dropping the stack of papers he starts to panic.

"Henri," he says, starting forward, "what are you doing?"

He empties the trash can underneath my desk and slaps my wrist with a terrified urgency I haven't seen in him before. We both watch as the pages fall to the bottom of the metal can and extinguish by themselves.

I look up to see that his face is wet with tears. I blink and realize mine is too.

"Henri," he says. "Henri. Henri, please." He grabs my shaking hand and pulls it down, our fingers intertwining. His voice breaks. "I can't do this. I'm sorry. I'm so sorry. But I can't…it hurts too much. I can't see you like this."

I look up at his tear-stained face, the curly strands of blonde hair shaking across his forehead. His glasses are fogging up. "I'm sorry," he whispers again.

"It's not your responsibility to fix me."

His shoulders cave in on himself and he drops to the floor, so this time it's me comforting him as he sobs.

"I don't know what to do," he says with a fractured tone.

"Then don't do anything."

"Henri, I can't just—"

"Yes, you can. You can and you will," I say. "Theo, this story didn't save me." I gesture to the trash can between us. "Stories have always saved me, but this one didn't. It didn't save her." He looks up at me, his eyes red and puffy. "If this didn't save me, I don't see how you can."

"You don't need to be saved."

I smile and shake my head at his naiveté. "You don't understand."

"No, I—"

"And you don't need to understand. You shouldn't. You have to go, Theo."

"Wh—"

"You have to go."

"Henri, please—"

"You have to go. I want you to go."

"Henri..."

"I mean it. I'm serious. I want you to leave."

"I can't."

"You have to, okay? I'm telling you to leave, Theo. I want you to leave. I don't want to see you ever again. I don't want to talk to you in class or outside of class and I don't want to be near you anymore."

He looks up at me, his heart splitting in front of my eyes.

And then he leaves me. Theo: the one thing keeping me

afloat. I watch his shoulder blades tense and then loosen as he opens and closes the door. He takes all the light with him.

"Henri?" Clary calls from the front door. "Are you home?"

She walks into the living room, untying her crochet scarf and hanging it up on a hook by the door. I watch as she sets down two paper bags and slips out of her coat. She sees me and gives a small smile.

"Hey. You get bored of your room?"

I shake my head and turn around, back to staring at the black coffee in the mug between my palms. I've been sitting like this for an hour, maybe more, and now the coffee is cold but I can't bring myself to heat it up or drink it.

"Henri?" Clary says. "Are you okay?"

She brings the bags to the kitchen and sets them on the counter.

"No," I say.

"Is it your book?"

"No."

"A class?"

"No."

She frowns. "Then what is it?"

"My—my mom died."

Her face falls. "What?"

"Yeah. I don't know. Dahlia called me earlier. Not earlier, I mean, a couple of days ago. I think."

"You...think?"

"I don't know."

"Okay," she says, her voice shaking. "Um. Are you okay? How are you doing?"

I shrug half-heartedly. "I don't know."

"Henri—"

"It's not the same. As when my dad died."

"Because you knew that was coming."

"I guess. But also I think I was angry at him so it felt kind of...fine. Just not terrible. Not like this." I look up at her and her eyes are as wide as a deer's. "That makes me sound atrocious, doesn't it."

"No. No, I think it's understandable. Maybe."

We share a melancholy grin.

"Have you told anyone else about it?" she asks.

I shrug and take a sip of the coffee to avoid the question. When I wince and cringe away from the mug, Clary takes it from my hands and pours it straight into the sink. She busies herself around the kitchen, heating water in a teapot and finding another chipped mug.

"You can talk to me, you know," she says. "I don't know what losing two parents feels like, but I know what losing one feels like."

"Yeah. I just...I just feel like it's kind of my fault." She turns back to me, her face heartbroken. "I feel like I could have saved her and I didn't. Because I knew Dahlia wasn't being nice to her and I knew it was hurting her more than she let on. And the alcohol, of course. The wine. That couldn't have been helpful. And after Dahlia called me, I just didn't know who to talk to. I didn't want to stress you out and my other friends aren't really...friends, and I couldn't talk to Theo about this because...well, I don't know. He's Theo. I didn't want him to see me like this."

"Like what?"

"Broken."

"Henri, you're not—"

"But it doesn't matter anymore."

"Why not?"

"He already saw me. And I ruined it."

"What? When did he come over?"

"Yesterday, I think."

"Yesterday?"

"Yeah."

"When?"

I give her a look. Why does she care so much about when Theo was here?

"I don't know. In the early afternoon? Around 10?"

She shakes her head. "Henri, I was here the entire day. No one came in."

"No, he came over. He brought me a book."

"Hang on, his name's Theo? Have I met him before?"

"No," I say, starting to get suspicious of her.

"What's his major?"

"Computer science."

She leans back, her face cold like stone. Her forehead creases and she rubs her temples.

"Henri, we don't have a computer science major here," she says heavily.

"No, Theo said—"

"I don't know who this guy is, but we don't have computer science at Woodbrick."

She's lying. She must be. There's absolutely no way Theo would have made something up like that.

"Okay, well, maybe I misheard him or something. But I've

been to parties and stuff with him. We went to a bakery together. And a McDonald's."

"What? Henri, you haven't gone to parties with anyone. You were always by yourself and didn't want me to come with you. Remember? You made me wait, like, five minutes after you left before I could come. And you went to McDonald's all by yourself. I had to come pick you up? Because your mom's car had run out of gas?"

"Huh? No, I went with Theo. He drove me. We went to a bookstore after."

"Yeah, where you bought a copy of *Wuthering Heights*?"

"How do you know that? I never told you that."

"Henri, you had it with you when I picked you up. You told me about it on the drive back home."

She's giving me a look I've seen only a few times before, mostly on Dahlia's face. *She's insane*, it says. *She's insane and she should be locked away. Why is she still here? Why is she still out?* But I'm not insane, because I know she's wrong and she's lying. She has to be; there is no other explanation.

"You're wrong," I say.

"Maybe..." She speaks gently, as if I'm some kind of toddler or a wounded animal. "Maybe your mom's death kind of...altered your memory. I don't know if it's possible, but, Henri, I don't know who you're talking about."

"He can't not be real," I half whisper. "It has to be real. It has to be."

"I don't...Henri, maybe you should see someone. A therapist? Because, I mean, these past few weeks, you've kind of been—"

"No," I say suddenly, standing up from the table. "I need to go for a walk."

"A walk? Is that a good idea? It's kind of cold right now, and it's getting dark out."

"Yeah, it's fine. I just need to think."

"Okay," she says uneasily. "But take a coat."

I nod and slide off the stool, retreating to my room to grab a sweater and a scarf. I rush over to the front door, where I pull on shoes, and leave Clary to wonder whether or not her roommate is actually insane.

The walk down to the lake is a quiet one. It's cold out, almost below freezing, and I only see a few people outside, probably walking to and from classes. My breath is visible in the gray air.

And despite the weather, the ground is still riddled with a mix of dirty snow and orange autumn leaves. I lean down and scoop a handful into a ball, chucking it at a nearby tree. It falls apart midair and barely touches the bark, but it feels good to throw something so I continue making snowballs and tossing them around as I walk closer to Lake George.

I used to go to the lake all the time last year. Eloise loved to go, mostly because it meant she could smuggle beer out there and be as loud as she wanted when she got drunk, and I would always tag along with her and the constantly changing group of boys who seemed to hang around her. I don't really miss those afternoons. Eloise would insist on sunbathing in our swimsuits, but I hated the way the material clung to my body even when it wasn't wet and I hated even more the stares of the guys she brought with her. I knew they were looking at her, not me, but it still didn't feel welcome.

So since then I haven't really gone. Which is a shame, because the lake is beautiful and I actually do enjoy going to sit on the sand and curl up with a book. I read *Walden* there, over the summer, and every time I went I felt a little more like Thoreau.

Lake George is just as pretty in winter as it is in spring and summer. Brackish orange and red is reflected off the clear water and the air even feels lighter, and of course the frogs make it better. Some of the braver ones splash in the shallow water near the shore but most of them are hidden behind logs and underneath bushes, croaking to their heart's content. I used to wish I could be a frog until I learned that all they eat is flies.

I've never been in winter and as I round the corner from the long, winding path it takes to get there I wonder why I haven't. The water doesn't freeze over, but it doesn't matter— the surrounding snow on the ground and in the trees makes it look like a tangible heaven. It's entirely still, entirely quiet, and everything is white.

Pulling my scarf tighter around my neck, I nudge the sleeves of my sweater over my freezing fingers and wish I'd worn something thicker as I clear off a nearby bench and sit down. I can already feel my pants beginning to soak through.

So I sit there and think about my fleeting sanity. I've already reached the conclusion that I am clinically insane, be-cause there is no other explanation for Theo and everything else. A part of me is fine with it, but then there's another part that's knocking from the inside of my chest and begging for me to stop before I go too far. *Too late,* I want to say to it. *I've already leapt off the edge, and I can't stop the fall now.*

Just as I think I've made peace with myself, a dark figure settles beside me. The man—I recognize him as an older version of my father, with a thick black beard on his jawline that he was never able to grow while he was alive partly because of chemotherapy but also because he just couldn't grow facial hair—stares out into the lake as I do. Without glancing at him I know we look alike; the slopes of our noses, the curve of our ears, the rolling tilt of our necks. I can never be rid of him.

"I thought you weren't coming back," I murmur.

He gives the lake a faint smile. "I thought I wasn't either." More snow falls off the edge of the bench as he readjusts, tapping his knee up and down. "But you didn't really give me a choice."

"I didn't?" I ask, amused now.

"No." He shakes his head. "You didn't."

"Did I call you back to me, or something? I don't remember ever wanting your help."

"You didn't call me. You can't do that," he says. "But I came for a different reason." He waits for a reaction from me, but when I don't give him one he continues on. "I know she's dead. I know she's gone." Traitorously my heart drops in my chest. "And I know it was Dahlia's fault. But what you don't realize, Henri, is that it was also your own fault. Just as much as hers."

"I don't—"

"I don't expect you to understand."

"So why are you here?"

He smiles, tilts his head to the side and looks upward at the clouds. It has begun to snow, I see, big flakes that drop with *patpatpat*s on the bench and in my hair and on the ground.

"I'm here to tell you that I was right," he says proudly. "That even though you never ceased to believe that literature would save you and everyone around you, you were wrong. It didn't save her. It didn't save you."

"I know."

"You have wasted years of your life for this. All of those hours, those words, all accumulated to nothing. No one read the one story you've ever finished before you destroyed it. What is your purpose now? What is the point of continuing to write if the very reason you wrote is gone?"

My voice shaking, I ball my hands into fists and shut my eyes tightly, willing him away. "She wasn't the only reason I wrote."

"Oh, I know. I was a big part of that, wasn't I? You needed an escape from the pain of losing the father you never knew. And Dahlia, of course. You needed to get away from her too. But the thing you never noticed, Henri, is that you were using stories to escape and get away from people, to retreat back into yourself. But you never considered that at a certain point maybe it isn't better to retreat into yourself. Because at one point you will come to despise yourself and your thoughts. And, then, what is the good of your mind when it's no more than a battleground? What is the good of your mind when it's no better than the outside?"

"What do you expect me to do? What else *can* I do?"

"Nothing," he hisses. "You can do nothing."

Tears are rolling down my face and they freeze midway. My nose, cherry red in the colorless air, starts to run and I sniffle incessantly. I know it's beginning to annoy my father.

"I tried to warn you," he continues. "I tried to tell you

this wouldn't amount anything, that literature has no real power in our world. But you wouldn't listen and your mother just encouraged the false reality."

"*What* do you want I to do?" I burst. "I can't stop. You don't understand, I can't just stop writing and forget about everything."

"Then don't. But you w drive yourself to madness."

"I'm already crazy. I'm talking to my dead father and I imagined an entire romance

"Then what will one more mistake be, in the grand scheme of things?"

I rub a wool arm over my nose and look at him. "What?"

"You feel betrayed."

"By who?"

"By what, you mean."

"No, I don't mean that."

"You feel betrayed by your words and other words and all the authors that have lived."

"I never said that," I protest.

"You didn't have to. Didn't I tell you earlier? I am you. You are me. You don't have to speak for me to know what you're thinking."

"Why won't you just leave me alone?"

"Because you do not want to be left alone."

"No, no, this is all wrong. This is all wrong. I have *friends*, I have people I can talk to. I don't need you."

"Do you really believe that? Would Eloise come running out here in the freezing cold for you to cry into her shoulder? No, I don't think she would. Did Clary care enough to try to stop you? No, she didn't. Be honest, Henri, you don't have anyone but me anymore. I have alvs been here, and I always will be."

Finally, I compose myself. Mack straightens, I inhale slowly, I brush my hair behind ears. The lake is silent as ever and my father, beside me, ws.

"You asked what else you can," he begins.

"Yes."

"And I'll tell you. You can plan end to literature. All that has been, all that will be. Wh good is it to anyone? It has not stopped any wars, it has n stopped injustice, it has not stopped death. It did not stoDahlia, and it did not inspire you to intervene. What is theoint, then?"

"I can't destroy every bookhat has ever been written."

"Maybe not, but you cantart here, at a college with one of the largest historical libraes in the western world."

"But what if—"

"Stop this nonsense, Hnri. Think of all the people you could save. Think of all te pain you could prevent. This rotten, unholy feeling coid up in your heart—no one else could have to feel it if youlo your part right now."

"I'd be helping other pople?"

"Yes. Of course. Of corse you would."

I pause.

"The library will be empty tomorrow night," he says. "They're closing it early, remember?"

"Yes."

"So you burn it down then."

"And if I get caught?"

"You will be caught. It is inevitable."

The recipe for arson is rather simple, actually. Black clothes, a jug (or two) of gasoline, a box of matches, the cover of darkness. And vacancy, of course. I'm not a murderer.

What I am is angry. Clary didn't ask why I was so late coming back to the dorm. If I had died out in the cold she wouldn't have cared. Eloise hasn't talked to me in weeks and I doubt she's noticed. Dahlia has also been avoiding me, not that I care. It's better if she does.

But they're all just proving what my father said, and now —with no more emotional attachments left—going to jail doesn't seem as daunting as it once did.

I spend my last day on campus burning up all my books with the window wide open. One by one, I toss them into my trash can and watch as the orange flames engulf them in flickering delight. As I set more and more on fire, I start to get excited for tonight, almost. I've never seen an entire building burn. But I can imagine its terrific beauty.

After I finish with the books in my room, I move on to the books in the living space Clary and I share. She's out at classes and with friends the whole day so I have free reign of the apartment. I want to applaud her stupidity.

She isn't back when night falls but I still change in my room with the door closed securely. I tie my hair up and secure it underneath a beanie, then slip my materials into a backpack and fasten it over my shoulders.

As I leave the room, I turn back for a moment. It looks different now that all the books are gone, but not in a bad way. It doesn't feel like the place where I used to live. It doesn't feel like the place where I wrote a story and then it failed me. It just feels like a room, and I'm ready to leave it behind.

I shut the door. The water-stained kitchen; the coffee-stained couch; the expansive window that overlooks campus. I'm ready to leave it all behind.

The walk to the library is short but dark. For some reason, the overhead lamps aren't turned on and the dirt paths are shrouded in darkness. Even better for me. The only sounds I hear are the dependable crunch of my shoes on snow and a nearby bird, singing somewhere in the trees. The dorm buildings let off an eerie glow, but other than that the only light is from the moon, which I stare up at for a while before continuing. Everything feels small when you're looking upwards.

The library looms over the courtyard, a gothic mass that leaves little to the imagination. It's exactly what you'd expect, complete with oak doors at the entrance, a ten-foot stained glass window, and a basement where the school stores precious historical documents. And it's all about to crumble to the ground.

I set my bag down near a maple tree and slowly take out the contents. First, the gasoline. I heave one jug into my arms and walk over to the side of the library, where I begin my pilgrimage around the building. It takes longer than I expected but I go back for another jug, set it down, and then go back for two more. I want to be thorough. The doors are locked so I take the liberty of smashing the windows before dousing the interior in the clear liquid. The alarms go off, blinking red in the darkness. I don't panic. The campus patrol takes a while to get around and they probably think this is just a prank some freshman pulled.

So I take my time returning to my bag for the final instrument. The box feels small and insignificant in my shaking palms. Shaking—why are they shaking? I look back at the library. From over here, it looks normal. The windows don't look shattered and the walls don't look gleaming wet.

My first few steps are slow. They get faster as I get closer. By the time I reach the front of the building I'm half-running.

I light the match.

The orange glow flickers into my eyes. I'm struck blind for a second.

What people don't talk about often is the beauty of a burning match. They talk about the fire, the flame, of course, but not the match itself. They don't talk about the eventual disintegration of the wood, the red curved tip that takes barely any time to succumb to the heat, the numbing pain as the fire gathers around your fingers. People don't mention the long, single strand of smoke that emerges. They don't talk about how it curls around air and fades upward.

But this is because people don't spend time standing around and staring at burning matches. They don't hesitate to light their candles or their cigarettes; they want to ignite it immediately without thinking about what they're doing.

And that's what I can't seem to stop doing: thinking about what I'm doing. It's especially hard to keep my thoughts straight when I feel a pair of eyes set on my back.

I turn.

"I can't do it."

"You can. You must," he says.

"But—"

"*Think* about it. *Think*. You remember her drunk on the bathroom floor. You remember her cowering underneath her youngest daughter. Will she die in vain? Will you not avenge her? Will you not terminate her murderer?"

The flame falls quickly through the air. The gasoline takes less than a second to ignite. Within a minute, the entire library has caught fire.

I step back uneasily, shuddering underneath the weight of what I have done. My father's arm keeps me from falling. He squeezes my shoulder as he stands next to me, calmly.

I pull away from him. I fall to my knees and cry as my father and I watch the library burn down. I cry for Dahlia, I cry for my mother, I cry for Theo, but most of all I cry for the death of literature and all the pain it has brought me.

Dear Mom:

I know you're not going to be able to read this. Or maybe, since you're looking down on people on earth (or looking up—I'm sure the lord you believed in knows you weren't a great mother) you can see everything they do. So maybe you can read this. But either way it doesn't really matter.

I've gotten a lot of questions about why I did what I did; why I burned down the library at my university, even though I was a student of literature. I never respond to those questions. They're pointless, honestly. Isn't the reason why I did it plain enough?

Maybe it's not. Or maybe people really are stupider than I thought.

I don't blame you for everything that's happened. Of course I don't. You'll never be able to understand that the cause of all of this was me, from the beginning, and art. I really do believe things could have been different if you'd kept me from writing and pursuing it. But I know I was uncontrollable, and I would have found a way around your rules eventually.

In court they asked me for my plea. I wanted to laugh right in the judge's face—did they really think there was any other answer besides guilty as charged? Because everyone saw me standing there after the library was gone. There are photos in the newspapers of me dressed in all black in front of the remains.

You wouldn't believe how many articles were published about me and what happened. I think people are fascinated with my position. They're saying I went mad. They're going to put me in their history books as a mad artist, as a raving lunatic.

But at least I'll be in their books. Because, I think, more than anything, I have always wanted to be extraordinary.

So maybe the real crime is that they didn't catch me sooner. Maybe it's that you, and Dad, didn't notice sooner. It wouldn't have been hard to, I don't think. My self-isolating tendencies were pretty self-explanatory. But to normal parents and a normal teenager, maybe. Not to you guys. Not to me.

A lot of people have said that I've thrown away my education, which makes me laugh even harder. Thrown it away? No, I used it. You know that, don't you? I used it to the full extent. All of my justification for this came from what I've learned, and I'm sure I'll join the long list of artists who lost their minds that someday a student like me will read about.

But despite all that—despite the list of artists and the pompousness of higher education and elite classes—there's something they don't tell you when you're learning about art history. Most of the artists you learn about are bad people. But me—not me.

I'm one of the good ones.

Love,
  Henri.

author's note

I started writing this book at fifteen years old and finished it at sixteen, and when I wrote the first line I had absolutely no idea what I was doing or what the story, at its core, was trying to say. That's probably not the best way to start writing a book. But after lots of discussion with my parents and more time spent inside of the story, its purpose became pretty obvious.

My generation is often criticized for being chronically online and is primarily known for the mental health crisis that is currently happening, but it's sometimes hard for older generations to truly understand what it feels like to know so much about the world at such a young age. Almost from birth we've been exposed to traumatic world events. We constantly hear about the horrors of war in places such as Ukraine and the Middle East, and some of us were born to parents who experienced the terror of 9/11. We lived through the global COVID-19 pandemic and have grown up hearing about school shootings nationwide, to a point where it almost feels inevitable to happen to every community. In recent years, the Opioid epidemic has reached students our age. All of this has occurred while we're continually being told about how our planet is dying and little is being done to prevent rising temperatures.

It's no surprise that my generation struggles with alarmingly high rates of depression and anxiety. I have seen this firsthand among my peers and friends, and have dealt with mental health issues myself.

As I wrote more of the first draft of this novella, I realized that the story I was trying to tell was concerned with the dangers of worsening mental states—especially if no one steps in to help. Henri's case is extreme, as she deals with undiagnosed mental disorders that most of the population does not have, but I think it can still serve as a reminder that mental health has a very real impact on the world.

The stigma around mental health has prevented necessary conversations we need to be having in our society. A part of the reason I wrote this is to create a space for this conversation to occur and to hopefully provide readers with a window into the mind of someone struggling with mental health issues.

So please do not take this story lightly—let it remind you to check in on your loved ones and to always be compassionate to others and yourself.

acknowledgements

Mrs. Mogilefsky, Mrs. Driver, Aunt Aida, Uncle Matthew, and Grace—thank you all so much for taking the time to read early drafts of this story and giving me incredibly valuable feedback and encouragement. This never would have been published without your help.

My sisters, Annie and Kate—I know you guys probably think I'm weird for wanting to sit in my room and write all day, but still, thank you for always supporting me and making me laugh even when I don't want to.

My parents—I love you both so much and hope you know how grateful I am for everything you do. Thank you for letting this dream become a reality.

about the author

Ella Sherry is a teenage author and poet from southern California. *The Art of Madness* is her first book.